Also by Laura Kasischke

Eden Springs

Eden Springs

(*A Novella by*
LAURA KASISCHKE)

14 13 12 11 10   5 4 3 2 1

Library of Congress Cataloging-in-Publication Data

Kasischke, Laura, 1961–
Eden Springs : a novella / by Laura Kasischke.
p. cm. — (Made in Michigan writers series)
ISBN 978-0-8143-3464-5 (pbk. : alk. paper)
1. House of David—Fiction. 2. Purnell, Benjamin Franklin, 1861–1927—Fiction.
3. Collective settlements—Michigan—Fiction. 4. Benton Harbor (Mich.)—Fiction.
I. Title.
PS3561.A6993E34 2010
813'.54—dc22
2009041884

Designed and typeset by Maya Rhodes
Composed in Fairfield LH, AT Old Fashion Script, and Myriad Pro
Picture frame image © Balaikin / Dreamstime.com

Although the quotations used at the beginning of each section are taken from actual documents and records, and the images are authentic, this novella is a fictional imagining of events, inspired by records and research on people and events. The author makes no claims to historical fact, and has taken great liberties with those facts for her story.

for
ED & JUNE KASISCHKE,
who told me the first stories

Contents

A Note on the House of David

In the spring of 1903, a preacher named Benjamin Purnell and five followers arrived in Benton Harbor, Michigan. They were "following a star" and fleeing a scandal. Within a few years, their message had spread across the world, and a thousand more followers of King Ben had joined those first five at his colony, which he named the House of David.

Benjamin Purnell was born in 1861 in Greenup, Kentucky, where he claimed to have been divinely inspired to gather a flock to await the end of the world, when he and his colonists would become the last living people on earth. At the Second Coming, they would be granted an "eternal life of the body," and would live together, in the flesh, forever.

For years the House of David itself must have been a kind of paradise. Its members, mostly young and healthy, built and lived in rambling mansions. It was said that the bricks from which the mansions were constructed had sand mixed into the mortar. They glittered in the sunlight. Proximity to Lake Michigan had tempered the climate for fruit-growing, and the colony was surrounded by orchards and vineyards. At that time, Benton Harbor shipped three million crates of fruit into the world annually. New colonists arrived monthly—by boat, by horse and buggy, by train.

In order to prepare their bodies for the Second Coming, members were told not to cut their hair, not to eat meat, not to engage in sexual relations. But accounts of the colony do not evoke a grim, chaste lifestyle. Reports of Purnell speak to an enchantingly handsome and charismatic man. It was said that if you had a dollar in your pocket when you met King Ben, he would have charmed you out of it before you parted. He liked music, dancing, and a good joke. It was said that he wore a white suit, rode a white horse, and was often seen in the company of beautiful girls dressed in white. A ruby locket hung around his neck. Although he was married (to two different women at the same time, by some accounts), he displayed great affection for all of his young female followers. They, it seemed, returned his affections, and the fervent loyalty the men in the colony gave to King Ben seems to have offered him the company of their wives, sisters, and daughters.

In keeping with his vision of creating in Benton Harbor a "Paradise on Earth," Benjamin Purnell began plans for an amusement park. In 1908 the Eden Springs Park opened. Eden Springs, over the decades, would become a major tourist attraction of the Midwest with its zoo, aviary, miniature train, beer garden, and musical and vaudeville acts performed in the amphitheater. The House of David baseball team became famous worldwide for the skill, the antics, and the beards of its players.

The contradictions between the preachings and the lifestyle of the colony did not go unnoticed. Here was a reputedly celibate Christian society, settled in the Midwest among farmers and businessmen, running one of the most popular and lucrative centers for recreation and entertainment in the country. They may have laid claim to an austere philosophy, but a vein of bliss and satisfaction seemed to run beneath it. The colonists were said to be attractive, quick to laughter, full of life. The men were skilled craftsmen, strong, hardworking, handsome. The women were extraordinarily beautiful, and their leader, Benjamin Purnell, seemed to be delighting in them. The colonists of the House of David may have been preparing their bodies for the Second Coming, but they seemed to be enjoying them fully in the meantime, along with the wealth and fame that Eden Springs brought.

In the end, it's a story not that different from the original story of the Garden of Eden. For a while there was pleasure and perfection, joy on earth and in the flesh, freedom, and perhaps a kind of innocence brought on by isolation and blind faith.

And the downfall—that much more terrible because it came to Paradise—was so full of sex and scandal it seemed to have invented death itself.

Today, a handful of elderly colonists continue to live in Benton Harbor. The mansions, most of them empty, still stand. The amusement park, closed down, remains where it was built—although it has been utterly claimed now by time and nature and decay. After his death in 1927, Benjamin Purnell's body was embalmed, and for decades it lay in state in a hermetically sealed glass coffin in the Diamond House, where he had lived for so many years with his "harem," until the house was vandalized by teenagers, the seal broken on the coffin, and the ruby locket stolen from around his neck. King Ben's followers, his girls, his persecutors, his defenders, and the tourists who once visited the amusement park, have scattered, have died.

Still, hundreds of weathered postcards survive, addressed by those long-gone tourists to friends and families. Those postcards bear excited messages of having glimpsed Benjamin Purnell strolling through the Eden Springs Park on a sunny day, like a god.

It was said that the occasional lady would faint when he passed.

He was known to have stopped now and then to kiss a particularly pretty visitor's hand.

Laura Kasischke

Prologue

SAYS HE BURIED GIRL IN CULT'S SAND PLOT

An inquiry by Sheriff Bridgeman of Benton Harbor, Michigan, revealed a gravedigger who told of receiving a frail, undecorated casket to bury with the information that it contained a 68-year-old follower of "King Benjamin" Purnell, and that her death was due to apoplexy. As he pushed the box into the grave the top broke off, revealing the body of a girl about 16, wrapped in old paper.

(*The New York Times*, April 29, 1923)

*Y*ou dig a hole in the sandy dirt, and you lower the casket into it. You shovel the dirt and the sand back over the box.

And all the time you're thinking about the sun on your back, or the rain. The sweat making stains on your shirt, the sound of a few crows screaming in the breeze, or you're thinking about a girl—your girl, someone else's girl—naked, posing, like in a postcard. Or you whistle the last song you heard, whatever song it was.

But there's a smell.

A silence, and a weight.

That silence is a weight, and you can't pretend you don't feel that.

So he looked away, angry at those crazies from the House of David for burying this old lady like a dog in a box as thin as paper, and nobody but him there to say a few words.

Nobody but him and the dead woman and the earth as far as the eye could see, the ear could hear. When he pushed it into the grave, the body tumbled out . . .

. . . brown paper, but then the paper tore away, and he

couldn't help looking right at her because she was looking at him.

He'd been told that she was sixty-eight. That all her people were over in England, or in Germany. Apoplexy, which he understood to be a blood-burst in the brain.

But this was no old lady staring back at him. This was a girl, no older than sixteen. Strawberry-colored hair in two loose braids; her lips were parted, and he could see her teeth, that they were dry and white. Except for the darkening grip of whatever it was that had killed her creeping down her neck, she could have been alive.

Blue-gray eyes.

He grabbed the shovel and started throwing sand on the open box—the girl with the strawberry-blonde braids, the torn brown wrapping paper—and all the time he could hear himself making choking sounds in his throat.

He was afraid someone would come by.

He was a gravedigger.

No one expects to see the gravedigger choking over a grave.

He left in a hurry, and when he passed a boy cutting weeds near the gate, neither of them said a word.

Part One

THEY ARE COMING FROM AUSTRALIA, ENGLAND,
IRELAND AND SCOTLAND BY FAMILIES

Are you satisfied to be a spirit—an angel—when you die, or do you want a material body? If you have a choice, the members of the "House of David," who have a colony at Benton Harbor, Mich., on a fine fruit farm of 800 acres, and are traveling over the world gathering converts, will instruct you.

Carriage No. 5, with Lulu, Grace, Frank, Myrtle and John, passed this way on an evangelizing tour of Ohio and Pennsylvania. Their faith, epitomized, is: "The end of the world is not far distant." Also, they say, if you let your body go down to the grave, then the best you can hope for in eternity is to be a flimsy, floating spirit, but those who have not died by the time of the second coming "shall return to the days of their youth, and their flesh shall become fresher than that of a child's."

(*Cleveland Press*, May 21, 1922)

ADMINISTRATION BUILDINGS.
HOUSE OF DAVID.

I *t was always a problem, what to do with a body. Cora*
Moon did the paperwork, but it was hard on her eyes.
The pen shook in her hand and splattered ink all over
the paper. There was something wrong with Cora, something recent, and related, most likely, to aging (anyone
could see that she wasn't what she'd been even the summer before: she could hear the young girls giggle that morning when, pouring tea, she splashed it on the table), and it
shouldn't have come as such a surprise. You couldn't even
drink a cup of milk you'd left on the table overnight. Or eat
an egg. Things spoiled. They decayed.

But Benjamin didn't want anything to do with that, and
they all listened to Benjamin, so the body was still out in
the orchard, and Benjamin forbade anyone to go near it.

"Let the dead bury the dead," he always said, taking it as a personal affront, death among the converts.

But he never told anyone how the dead could bury the dead.

They were supposed to live forever.

This was, after all, his paradise. He'd made promises concerning eternal life and committed those promises to writing.

When a boy came back to the house and said he'd been watching "a sky so full of vultures over the orchard that it was like night," Cora said something had to be done or they were going to get in trouble with the state, and Benjamin said, "Okay, okay, old lady," and finally sent Paul Baushke out there with a wagon and some pine boards and a handful of nails.

Baushke built the coffin right around the body and then drove it over to the cemetery for the gravedigger to take.

But that, Cora knew, would not simply be the end of that. There would be questions and paperwork and who knew what else, and Cora was the one who was going to have to worry about that.

Lena McFarlane watched out of the corner of her eye as Cora's hand shook over the paper and splattered ink at the edge of it, and even on the table.

"What are you going to write down there, how she died?" Lena asked, trying to make it sound like she didn't, herself, care one way or the other.

Cora didn't say anything, so Lena stood up and looked over the old woman's shoulder.

"Struck by lightning!" Lena clapped a hand over her mouth and laughed out loud.

Cora put the pen down and made her hand into a fist—partly out of anger but also because the hand was so tired. There was a dull ache in the center of her palm. She turned around to frown at Lena, but the girl was already gone, just the swish-swish of her long skirts as she hurried out of the office and into the hall.

Benjamin is of medium height, rather slenderly built and has an extremely fine face. His hair hangs down on his shoulders in long silken curls . . . His features are aquiline and well formed. His manner is gentle. His hands are white. Every movement is of a man at peace with himself and the whole world. He teaches and preaches gentleness. His followers listen to his voice as though it were the voice of a deity . . .

(*The Detroit News*, April 2, 1905)

*M*yrtle Sassman was sewing a baby bonnet in the shade when Lena ran past laughing about something, holding her skirts up over her ankles as she ran.

It was spring, and all at once for a while everything was in bloom at the same time—the lilacs and the dogwood and the orchards.

The orchards!

Mile after mile of perfume and light.

Soon there would be serious work to be done—long afternoons on ladders in the sun—but now things were just beginning again, starting out slow and luminous, the way they'd always begun.

Myrtle could see that Lena wasn't wearing shoes, just running over the grass in her stocking feet.

Lately Lena was always laughing about something. Sly little laughs. High, small cacklings. She was the prettiest girl in the Colony at the moment (and how briefly those moments came and went—the children growing, spring, the dogs out back of the kitchen devouring the scraps like wolves, the prettier girls growing older every day), and Lena knew it. All that shiny hair. Her pale skin.

It was a surprise, that beauty. Most of them remembered when Lena had been born, dark blue and reeking of wine. They'd locked Lena's mother in the attic while she was pregnant, to keep her from getting drunk and falling down the stairs, but she'd found her way to the wine anyway.

Not long after that, Lena's mother died, and they all expected the infant Lena to slip away, too, because she wouldn't take another nurse and was too stubborn to drink from a bottle or a spoon.

"She's used to the wine in her mother's milk—" Cora Moon finally understood, and they started to mix a bit of the communion wine with her milk, or wine and water mixed into a thin sweet gruel.

And she didn't die.

After she turned five, she wasn't even cross-eyed.

It was as if life had gotten a grip on that girl and turned her into a prize. They took to calling her the Sunshine Child around the Colony because of her flaxen hair.

Now she was running down the slope toward the amusement park, probably on her way to spread some gossip or to tell a lie. Because she was so pretty and had been sickly, because she was so lazy and slow and no good at anything, Lena didn't have to work like the other girls did. Her leisure was a dangerous thing.

Myrtle inspected the tiny white stitches under her hands—a perfect silky row, smooth against the cotton. Two months left to sew booties and bonnets. When the baby kicked her hard in the ribs, Myrtle gasped.

The band was playing, and Benjamin came walking toward us all dressed in white. I thought I was entering paradise . . .

(H. Pritchard, convert)

Benjamin loved girls.

To him, we were like fruit. To us, he was like God. He told us if we believed in him we would live forever—not just in spirit but in the flesh. When the end came, we'd have our young bodies back again, exactly as they were. Slim, unfreckled, fragrant. And it seemed more than possible. It seemed likely. As likely as the life that we were living then.

Those years, those days, the sky was always blue above the orchards—and the abundance! There was so much, even the jays didn't argue about the cherries. Instead, they darted in and out of the branches overhead as if they were sewing an intricate curtain of lace in the air between their nests. Or a bright wedding dress that floated on the breeze. The end seemed very near, as tangible as light, and we sang hymns as we worked.

Every afternoon he'd come to visit us in the orchard just as the sunlight was whitest, pouring itself into the air like milk into a glass of water, floating in fluid strands, weightless as hair. We could hear the hooves of his horse before he reached us—the ground shaking as if something under it were being born—and by the time he got to us we'd have our aprons straightened, the bows of our sun hats tied neatly beneath our chins.

We wore white because it was cool, soothing to the bees, and because the wearing of black was forbidden.

He taught us what to wear, what to eat, how to walk across the grass, between the trees, as softly as God walked on the earth, taking only what was needed or most desired, not even leaving a footprint behind us in the dust.

So the bees didn't sting, they only circled the sweetness to smell it, and the sound of them was like the low drone of bright tiny angels in our hair, and when Benjamin, our leader, smiled, the hard work seemed easy. He laughed at the palms of our hands stained red, and that white horse he rode bareback would paw impatiently at the ground.

Even as a tiny child Benjamin was given to religious matters. I would watch him out back when he thought no one could see him, and he'd be preaching to the trees.

(Elizabeth Purnell, mother)

*C*ora *Moon gave the certificate to Benjamin to sign.* She'd changed cause of death to "Apoplexy" and age of deceased to "68" after Lena laughed out loud at "Struck by Lightning."

He was sitting by the window in his room, holding a book with tiny print up to the light to read it, and when she took the paper from him he smiled shyly.

He must think I know he's scared, she thought.

Scared of the state. Scared of the dead. Scared, she supposed, of her, of what she might know.

And her failing eyesight and trembling hands probably scared him, too. The skin loose on her neck. The whiskers she couldn't see well enough to pluck out of her chin. Everybody knew that "Never Grow Old" was Benjamin Purnell's favorite hymn. He liked to sing it and accompany himself on a Hawaiian mandolin.

What must he think of her now?

Benjamin took charge of his face. "Thank you, Cora," he said. "I 'preciate your taking care of things."

It was his kind way of asking her to go away.

"Miss Moon?" the boy, Benjamin, so long ago, asked.

His voice came from behind her. She was erasing the chalkboard because the girl whose punishment it had been to erase it had run out the door after school before there was time to remind her. The reason for her punishment was that she could never remember to do anything unless she was reminded.

Cora saw that, despite all her teaching, some of the children—their stringy hair hanging over their eyes, tongues stuck out while they did their thinking—didn't know how to hold a pencil and wouldn't know how to hold a pencil by the time they were seventeen. It didn't matter what she did or didn't do. There were all those eyes and eyelashes, and she wanted to try, but she also knew she could only save a few, if she managed to save any at all. She knew, too, that the ones who would be saved—the ones who wouldn't die never having read a book from its beginning to its end or knowing how much change the manager of the General Store owed them—those ones could have been taught by any teacher.

The uppercase, the lowercase, the printing, and the cursive. The names of the presidents. The multiplication tables. The branches of government and the queens of England, only so they could be farmers like their fathers, suffer, maybe even die in childbirth like their mothers.

"Miss Moon?" Benjamin, the boy, asked again. "May I speak with you?"

"Benjamin," Cora said. "Of course, sit down, young man. You weren't in school again today."

In fact it had been weeks since she'd seen him, except to pass him in the street. She'd heard he'd taken to preach-

(18)

ing about Jesus, that there'd been singing and fainting, and that he'd been baptizing folks from all over Fleming County in the creek. Such things were common as mud in Greenup, Kentucky. Travelers came through all the time with their Bibles and a few girls playing tambourines, and soon there were visions and prophecies, and half the county was seen at some point or other wading out into the creek with a preacher—although most gave up the faith by spring, until the fall, when another preacher would come around.

Still, it was unusual to have one of your own people turn to preaching right in his own place. Usually, if a preacher wanted to find an audience, he had to leave his town where everybody knew him just as the son of the drunkard, or the boy who used to snitch things from the General Store, or the grandson of Old Joe Fogarty who hanged himself in his barn. But the gossip in Greenup—that breezy scarf that wound round and round them all, sewn out of boredom and fear—said that Benjamin Purnell had been hammered directly on the head by God.

(That boy's been set afire.)

(That boy's got a message from the Lord.)

You had to hear what he had to say for yourself.

"I'm fine, Miss Moon," Benjamin said. His hair had grown longer since she'd last seen him, and in the dim light of the schoolroom it looked redder than it had been, too. There was a veil of chalk between his face and hers, hanging and shining in the air.

He said, "I'd like to tell you something."

Cora could smell sweat on him, sweet and salty. What was he now—sixteen?

He was growing into his body, and it was easy to imagine the younger girls and the lonely older ones—the widows and the spinsters and the disappointed brides—throwing themselves into the Old Town Creek with him, their hair dripping down their backs. It was easy to imagine the crayfish, the sharp rocks, the rusty water rolling over their feet and up their ankles like cold silk stockings, and him making the sign of the cross on their foreheads with his fingers.

Cora had seen plenty of such preachers, but she had not, herself, followed into any water after them.

Being a teacher meant always keeping an eye out for cheaters, for tricks. Having dedicated herself to coaxing others out of their ignorance, she was naturally suspicious, and hard to make a fool of, and she didn't, anyway, go following men anymore. She'd come to Greenup, Kentucky, from the larger town of Eveleen after her mother had died and the man she was intended to marry, Morris McDonald, had announced his engagement to Mabeline Bowen, the prettiest girl in town.

And now Cora was forty-three—seven years older than her mother had been when she died—and despite her strong limbs and narrow waist and gold hair that refused to go gray, she was considered a very old woman who would never marry and certainly never have a child. Already pretty Mabeline Bowen was dead and gone, along with Morris McDonald and their two daughters, buried somewhere together on a grassy hill in Eveleen (the sun shifting itself over them all and the breeze making shady waves in the green and only a few crows cawing through the silence from tree to tree). One bad winter over a decade ago took them all together of a lung disease while, for Cora Moon, life went on and on.

As Benjamin sat down across from her, Cora waved a hand in the chalk-dusty air between them so she could see him better, and he sneezed.

"God bless you," she said.

He took out a very clean handkerchief and blew his nose. It gave her a chance to look at his hands, which were the hands now of a man, but, like his handkerchief, very clean. Trimmed nails. Knuckles scrubbed clean. He had to be the cleanest young man she'd ever seen. Perhaps the only clean young man she'd ever seen in Greenup, Kentucky.

Yes, she could see it clearly—how easily the girls of Fleming County, the pretty along with the homely in their white baptismal robes, would be guided into the cold ankle-deep water of the Old Town Creek by his hand, and how the first bone-chill of that water would come as a terrible surprise, but then the lying back, and the deafness under it, and then the being raised back up sputtering into his arms, the sign of the cross made slowly on your damp forehead by that clean hand.

"God bless you, too," Benjamin said and tucked the handkerchief back into his pocket.

"What did you wish to discuss?" she asked.

Benjamin took a deep breath then, and for a moment Cora was afraid that he might start to sing, but instead he spoke to her in such a soft voice she had to lean forward in her seat to hear him.

"I get these messages," he said, "about Paradise on Earth. And I can see it. Full of temples. And the temples have names from out of the Bible. Jerusalem, the Ark, Bethlehem, Shiloh. They're shiny. Splendid. Like from an olden time. And people are coming to see them from all over the world. The people are laughing. And there's birds in cages. And music—trumpets—and beautiful girls, like angels, and people working, and entertaining, and there's games in the summer, like baseball, and in winter skating on a lake. We're not worried about anything, and it goes on forever, and it never ends, and, Miss Moon—"

He leaned forward himself and looked her so closely in the eyes she was afraid that if she blinked she might fall to the floor, or forward, into him, so she held his gaze, not even breathing, and he even blushed when he said, smiling, so close to her face she could see the thin film of spit on his bright teeth, "And you're there, too, ma'am, and I see you dancing there, in the shade of a nice tree, on a green lawn, wearing a big white dress, and I'm twirling you about in my arms."

His complexion is clear, pink and white, and his eyes are blue and clear. His manner is gentle and well bred . . . His followers eagerly drink in every word he says and believe implicitly that he has been sent to lead the world . . .

(*The Detroit News*, April 2, 1905)

Nights.

Nights, he'd gather us around him. His Beauties, he called us. His Mighty-Cuties.

Nights were a simple pleasure.

There were whole skies full of stars and dangers a house could hide you from—blue-black clouds full of thunder. The wind. Sometimes it screamed like a girl.

Some nights he read to us from the Bible.

Some nights he told us stories and laughed like a madman.

But every morning the sun came up, and there'd be little heart-shaped tracks in the rose beds, or in the snow—some harmless animal that came out to circle the Diamond House in the dark.

We shall not all sleep. And this mystery is without controversy . . . God manifest in the flesh—not dead flesh nor corruption. He is the God of the living.

(Benjamin Purnell)

*M*yrtle Sassman *first glimpsed Benjamin Pur-nell* out back, behind her father's barn.

It wasn't the first time a preacher had come to the Sassman farm. Myrtle's father had a reputation in town. Food and money. He'd give them to any man who could talk fast enough or give him a bit of company in the winter or in the long weeks that came before spring, those weeks when he had a farmer's prophetic dreams—snakes in the eggs, a stillborn lamb, an owl eating a litter of new-born kittens in the barn. Strange beasts sniffing around the back door. Black furless things with forked tails. Birds lined up on the branches of bare trees, calling his name.

"Yes," Myrtle's father said to the preacher, wiping his hands off on the seat of his overalls, "life of the body," as if he, too, had been thinking about this.

The preacher took his hat off to nod seriously, and sun shone all over his hair then, and Myrtle thought she caught a whiff of wood smoke—spicy and clean—which rose over him into the air and mixed with the vinegar smell of chick-ens. There was a gold ring with a red stone on the middle finger of the preacher's right hand, and the stone appeared deep to her, deeper than a stone, swallowing the light.

Standing before him in his dirty overalls, Myrtle's father seemed childlike. Hopeless, and desperate with hope.

"Could we offer you something to drink?" he asked, and the preacher nodded.

"Myrtle, go fix the preacher some tea."

"Myrtle," the preacher said. "A fine name for a girl."

And the way he said it made her feel warm, sleepy, as though she'd been drinking wine, as though she'd never heard her own name spoken aloud before.

In the kitchen, Myrtle poured tea into her mother's favorite teacups for her father and the preacher, who had come in behind her. They sat down at the table, and the preacher spread a sheaf of photographs—mansions, girls in white dresses, men with flowing beards and hair to their waists—before her father, and then Myrtle went into the next room and pretended to sew up a hole in a pair of her father's pants.

She listened.

The chair she sat in was hard against her back. Winter was coming, and the wind through the cracks in the walls and between the windows and their frames whistled ominously, a tune she'd heard before and had been hearing for thirteen Novembers, the same tune they'd been whistling while her mother withered upstairs under a quilt she'd pieced together herself only the spring before.

Her mother's death-cries were in that whistle, even now. Wee—ee—ee—ee on the other side of the heavy curtains, and then that cold, snaking around Myrtle's ankles, singing.

But in the kitchen, her father and the preacher were laughing.

"Myrtle!" her father called loudly, as if she were much farther away than she was. "Go fetch the Bible. Brother Benjamin wants to read some pieces to us."

Myrtle fetched the Bible from the hallway, blew the dust off the cover, brought it to the kitchen, and placed it on the table in front of the preacher, who gestured for her to sit beside him. He opened it almost perfectly to the page he wanted and placed his finger elegantly on the verse, and Myrtle watched the side of his face as he read from their old Bible, mildewed and misshapen from years of lying under a dressing table, collecting things. Myrtle's mother had stuck flowers and leaves in it. Snippets of Myrtle's baby-hair. There was a scrap of wedding dress in it. And other scraps: A bit of black. A bit of pink. "Ye shall not round the corners of your heads, neither shalt thou mar the corners of thy beard."

Myrtle's father ran his fingers over his bare chin as the preacher read, and Myrtle looked at the preacher's beard.

"No cutting of the hair whatsoever?" Myrtle's father asked when he was done reading.

"None whatsoever," the preacher said. He had perfectly clean fingernails. Myrtle had never seen anything like it. He drummed his fingers on the pine table in time to his own rhythmic reading. Something about the selling of possessions and goods. Something about suffering and living forever and bodies shining. Within a week after Benjamin Purnell's visit, Myrtle's father wrote a note, which he left nailed outside the Dry Goods Store in town:

GONE TO BENTON HARBOR
FOR THE LORD CALLS
SASSMAN FARM LAND AND ANIMALS
GIVEN FREELY TO THEM WHO NEEDS EM

It took seven days and nights to get from the farm in Illinois to the House of David, and everywhere they stopped along the way they'd tell of the new home to which they traveled. They were going to live forever. The body would not perish but be returned to the days of its youth, the skin made fresher than that of a child's, the blood in their bodies transformed to spirit. When the end came, the House of David in Benton Harbor, Michigan, would be the only safe place on the face of the earth.

Some people would lower their eyes, in the presence of childish fools, and others would listen.

Myrtle had taken the Bible, and they'd packed their clothes and a few things that had belonged to her mother, and they'd hitched the big brown draft horse to the wagon and let him haul them toward their new life.

Slowly.

That horse had never before left the field behind the Sassman farm where he had been born, and now he wanted to stop every few miles to look around, to gather it in before he plodded on. When he stopped, Myrtle's father would put his hands on his knees and sigh. There was no sense trying to budge that horse if he wasn't ready to go. When he started up again, Myrtle watched his big buttocks shivering with muscle. Stubbornness, made of meat. In the mornings, it was cold, and she could see that horse's breath pour out of his nostrils like smoke.

Nights, they slept as close to the road as they could so they could hurry on again as soon as they woke. For dinners, she made a custard out of milk and eggs and brown sugar they'd brought from home, stirred it with a tin spoon that turned to silver in the moonlight, and kept stirring until what was in the pan changed from milk and eggs into something warm and solid, a thin membrane of sweetness floating on the top.

Digging into it, her father was all lit up in the cooking fire. Only once, he asked, "Myrtle, have we done right?" Beyond them, an owl in a tree said something to a mouse—*Who? You!*—and the sky, unfathomably deep and dark, was twinged with stars and clouds that looked like thin rags between Myrtle and the moon.

"Yes, Daddy," she said, without bothering to take a breath before she said it, because it was what a daughter said, and because she didn't need to think about it to believe it, and in the morning they packed their things again and headed north.

God did not give us flesh that we might feed it to worms.

(Benjamin Purnell)

ISRAELITE COLONY VIEW
Benton Harbor, Mich., U.S.A.
Send for literature.

*C*ora Moon knew the children in Greenup, Kentucky, thought she was old. And folks in town. Something about a teacher, she supposed. You have always been old. You were born old. A schoolteacher embarrasses people who've never been to school or who did poorly there. And a female schoolteacher especially embarrasses the men. Maybe they think you're angry with them or that you know something they don't know. They need to dismiss you. You're not a person, certainly not a woman.

But it always surprised her that even Old Man Craycroft, from whom she rented her room in town, never bothered her.

Old Man Craycroft—who was generally considered a danger to every female in the county since his wife had passed away, who'd wait outside the General Store all day if he thought Lillian Garnett or Minnie Rogers might come by (neither one of them more than a year or two younger than Cora Moon)—was never anything but polite to Cora.

"Hello, ma'am. How are you, ma'am?"

And that seemed somehow terrible. She blushed each time he called out to her so kindly, as if he'd slapped her behind.

Cora Moon had a figure that neither Lillian nor Minnie had—six to ten children between them (who could keep count?), and their bodies had fallen to ruin while Cora's was still sharp, erect, and slim. Although she kept her hair done up in a bun with a bit of black ribbon wound around it during the day, the hair was very blonde, still, and at night she brushed it out until gold sparks flew all around her reflection in the mirror. She had hardly a line on her face (all those years in the schoolroom), yet Old Man Craycroft called after her every time he saw her, as if she were a nun or his elderly aunt, "Good day, Miss Moon," and he never failed to take his hat off in her presence.

Benjamin paused in his chair in the schoolroom, as if to see if he would be allowed to continue.

"Go on, Benjamin," Cora said.

"Miss Moon," he said, "I think this vision is a sign from God concerning you."

The sound of the creek splashing past outside. It was April, still a week until Easter.

Had she not also had visions? Seen signs?

On her walk to the school that very morning, she'd seen a dead frog in a ditch, and the frog seemed oddly colored—red and pink, glowing in the sunrise—lying on its back, belly to the sky. One of its legs had been torn away.

By a bird?

There were several crows at the side of the road flapping their wings but not flying away.

And that frog had cast a strange pall over the rest of the morning. As the children were taking their tests—the younger ones adding numbers under ten together, the older ones answering questions about a chapter of their history book about Mary, Queen of Scots—Cora Moon had watched the tops of their heads and thought about all the children who must have sat in those very chairs (it was an old schoolhouse, and in all of its years, to her knowledge, not a piece of furniture had been changed or even rearranged) as a string of other teachers looked on.

And where were those teachers now, and where were those school children?

That spring day, the dead flies on the windowsill had come back to life.

Spring, every year, and the flies and flowers and fruit returned. Was that not God telling His people something in symbols and signs? Those flies were buzzing and bumping blindly against the glass, alive again that morning, and the whole room filled up with the noise of flies as the children stared down at their tests.

She'd noted it then, hadn't she, although she hadn't allowed herself to understand it until now?

Suddenly she was afraid and stood up from her chair, which made a terrible scraping sound on the floor. She'd lived in Kentucky her whole life, and she knew all about signs and the things they made people do. When she was a child, there was a tree split into three pieces by lightning in a field one spring night, and although the family to whom the field belonged had lived on that land for generations, within a few days they'd packed up their things and moved away in three pieces—the father and a son gone north, the mother and another son gone south, and two older sisters headed west together. They said it had been obvious from the tree and the lightning that this was what God wanted, and no one had questioned the wisdom of their decision. Even Cora Moon's father, who was a practical man, hadn't doubted the violent, incontrovertible sign. Cora, who was only nine and had never contradicted her father before, said, "But, Daddy—" The expression on his face had kept her from saying anything more.

Benjamin said, "Miss Moon, in addition to my dreams, this afternoon on my way to visit you, I saw a snake in the dirt, and it was sleeping in the shape of a *C*."

Eighty-three solemn, dreamy-eyed, slow-talking men, women, and children, who style themselves "The Living Roll of Life" and the "Israelite House of David," and who declare that they are direct descendants of the Lost Tribe of Israel, reached New York yesterday morning on the North German Lloyd liner Princess Irene, from Naples. They are bound for Benton Harbor, Mich., where they say they will await the millennium.

(*The New York Times*, March 24, 1905)

ISRAELITE COLONY VIEW
Benton Harbor, Mich., U.S.A.
Send for Literature.

*I*t was the third week of May when Myrtle and her father reached the House of David, and the orchards were in bloom—miles of pink trees, then miles of white, then miles of pink and white on either side—and it was like traveling into heaven. The air was sparked with petals, which fell into their hair. Her father's hat was covered with those petals. He was unshaven, and there was a ring of sweat and dirt around his collar, a hole in one of the knees of his black pants. And Myrtle's apron, which had belonged to her dead mother, was soiled with custard and ashes.

But the farm seemed more than two hundred miles away, seemed to Myrtle Sassman like another life, a life that was over finally and had begun again in Paradise.

Part Two

IMPORTANT NOTICE

Owing to the desire of many to come to the House of David faster than we are able to build and prepare for them, we wish it understood by all such that in order to save us and themselves much unnecessary trouble, that they should correspond with us before making arrangements to come.

(*Shiloh's Messenger of Wisdom*)

*L*ena left the door to the *Diamond House* open behind her, and the afternoon light poured into the waxed and formal darkness of the parlor. She tiptoed into the kitchen, where Estelle was whistling "Skip to My Lou" and punching at a loaf of dough, her braids all loose and floury behind her.

When Lena got close enough, she reached out and grabbed Estelle around the waist with one arm and put a hand over Estelle's gasping little mouth. She quit whistling fast.

"Don't scream," Lena said in a low voice, pretending to be him, "or I'll pull up your skirts and take you right now."

"Lena!" Estelle snapped when she managed to struggle away from her.

And it was a struggle.

Lena was stronger than Estelle, who was small as a doll—seventeen, but could have passed for twelve. In her anger and embarrassment, Estelle's cheeks were brilliant pink. The flour that had been on her hands was all over the yoke of her dress now, and she was panting.

"Lord. God. Are you plain crazy, Lena? You scared me half to death, and look—you tore a button off my blouse."

There was a gap in the floured white cloth of Estelle's dress where Lena could see a bit of her flour-white flesh.

"Sorry, sweetheart," Lena said, still in Benjamin's voice. "Maybe a big kiss'll make you forgive me." She stepped toward Estelle with her arms open and then grabbed Estelle's arm when she tried to get away, pulled her back, kissed her on the mouth.

The kiss was fast, and mostly bumping teeth, but Estelle staggered away, wiping her mouth with the back of her hand, tears in her eyes. "You're wicked," she said, looking hard into Lena's eyes, holding up a hand to keep her away.

"Yep," Lena said, and put a hand on her hip. "But you know what else is wicked?"

Lena could see the girl was trembling. The big kitchen was filled with humid and yeasty air. The dough on the counter had begun to rise again, and there wasn't the slightest imprint of Estelle's last punch in it.

"What else is wicked," Lena went on, "is Miss Moon writing on Elsie Hoover's death certificate, *Struck by Lightning*."

Estelle just stared, still with that hand held up to keep Lena back. Her eyes were very pale and rather small, and Lena liked to think they made Estelle look plain and dumb despite her rosebud mouth and the lightness of her tiny feet when she danced or ran.

"Well," Estelle finally said, "being as you weren't there, what do you know?"

Lena laughed and shook her head. She said, "Well, I know there's a slim chance a girl got struck by lightning in the middle of the orchard on a sunny afternoon. I guess I do know that."

Estelle narrowed those tiny eyes, and then she turned her back. "Lena," she said over her shoulder, sounding weary. "I've had enough of your nonsense, and if you bother me any more I'll get Cora, or Brother Vaughn. I don't got to put up with this. I got twelve loaves of bread to bake today, and since I know you got nothin' to do, why don't you either help me or get out of the way?"

Lena smiled at Estelle's back and said, "Well, I guess I'll just get out of your precious way," and then she turned and pretended to skate in her stocking feet across the kitchen floor before turning again and saying to Estelle's stiff spine, "Besides, who says I got nothing to do today?"

Q. What representations did they make to you?

A. That they were living as one family. That it was the only place to make eternal life; they represented that I would live forever.

(Harry Williams's statement, Nichols trial notes)

*C*ora *Moon had accounting to take care of, but her* mind was on other things.

The past.

A sky.

Blackberries.

She remembered picking them from a bush, dropping them one by one into a pail.

But where was that?

They did not grow blackberries here. The money was in cherries, grapes, and apples. Some peaches. Some plums. The pears.

Let the earth bring forth grass, the herb yielding seed, and the fruit tree yielding fruit after his kind, whose seed is in itself, upon the earth: And it was so.

She put down her pencil, thinking of something else, something long ago. A hot and buggy afternoon, but she'd been happy. She was a child. The sunlight was pale yellow, pouring itself into the sky like paint into a glass of water. In the trees above them, blue jays darted back and forth, screaming. It was as if they were busy sewing something between them.

A wedding dress. A curtain.

When was that?

She picked up her pen again, and wherever that had been, whoever she'd been then, was gone.

And her hand. This hand. It was an old woman's hand. Some strange old claw.

Was it still hers?

Cora laughed at herself, at that, but it sounded far away and dry.

No one wanted to grow old.

No one wanted to die.

That was Benjamin's religion. His vision. The youthful body, the joy of being in it. It had come to him in a flash one day, he said, like lightning, when he was still a boy:

There is no death, the lightning said.

It was spring then, too, and there was noise. Squirrels chattering. Birds screaming. He said he dropped his composition book in the mud before he got to the end of the dirt road on which he lived with his mother—but when he went back for it, none of the pages had even gotten wet.

For years he'd heard the preacher talk about hell, he said, the coming ruin. Fire, maggots, ashes to ashes. But after the lightning, wiping the muddy water off the back of his composition book, Benjamin realized that it was something else entirely.

There was no life without a body, without a body in the world—this body, this world, this dirty road, this rain, this particular smell of greenness in this particular breeze. It wasn't supposed to change, or end. It made sudden, new sense to him, and when he spoke of it, it made sense to other people. For many, it was the first thing they ever remembered believing. And they believed.

Cora had believed. It made lovely sense of everything.

Once she'd eaten a spoonful of mashed potatoes that had a needle in it. Too late, she'd remembered the embroidery her sister had been doing in the kitchen, and the needle. Its mysterious disappearance. And that quick glimpse of a glinting something in the spoonful of potatoes. She could even taste it on her tongue, but before she could stop herself from swallowing, the needle was gone, and Cora felt it slipping down her throat—the bright taste of it still in her mouth.

She was sixteen. She told no one. She went on with the meal and the cleaning up, and she sat near the fire darning socks that night and said goodnight to her father as she always did before she went to bed.

It wasn't until she was alone in the dark that she let herself think about the needle inside her, where it was, how it was doing its work deeply, invisibly, inside of her—a secret between them. And she'd been ready for whatever would happen next. The pain. The death. The end of everything.

But she never felt the needle again.

If it passed through her, she never noticed. If it was still inside her, it had become a part of her—a promise the two of them were always keeping. Usually, now, she didn't think of it at all. She was an old woman. Who knew how many needles she'd eaten?

Now she stood up from the accounting altogether and went to the window, looked out at the spring weather rolling across the lawn, and she put her hand to her throat and thought of Benjamin telling a crowd of men and women with long hair standing in an orchard in the twilight of a spring evening, "Someday this place will be Paradise. God will be here, walking among us, followed by his angels. The gates will be made of diamonds. There will be no more sickness, old age, death. Those who believe in it will be here. We will be here forever, living together in beauty and peace."

It still seemed possible then—and, like all the others, she'd loved the sound of his voice, and Cora could imagine, easily, the diamonds blazing in the gates.

How it would always be spring.

There had been a stiff breeze that evening through Eden Springs, and Benjamin's white hat had blown off his head, and there had been chaos and laughter as some young boys chased after the tumbling whiteness in the dying day. Hatless in the breeze, Benjamin did a little dance to entertain the crowd until the boys brought it back, bowing to him, and then he went on:

"Someday," he said, trying to regain the seriousness he'd lost, "we won't have to pray to speak to God, because God will be right here."

Those early years in Benton Harbor, the forests around the town were still dense, always trying to creep back in, to take over again. Picking fruit, Cora and the others saw bear cubs at the edge of the orchards, sniffing around, making throaty human sounds. Huge birds would beat suddenly out of the shadows, screaming. There were eyes every morning between the trees if you peered in to see them, seeing you.

Laura Kasischke

So much beauty, so much plenty.

They were left alone. No one seemed to know or care why the House of David was there. They were good neighbors. They wore white. They let their hair grow. Who could complain about that? They were polite. They kept to themselves, except when there was trouble in the town—fire, accident, illness—when they'd be the first to offer help.

In the middle of the second summer, the Australians arrived. Having heard the word, they came and brought with them a wallaby, a kangaroo, a whole cage of exotic birds. Cora stood beside Benjamin and watched them marching up the middle of the road, already with their long hair flowing, and some of the House of David boys ran back for their instruments, struck up a hymn, and the girls joined hands and danced on the front lawn of the Diamond House, and Benjamin waved an American flag, and the Australians wept in his arms and kissed his hands and bowed before him.

It was the kangaroo that gave Benjamin the idea to start a zoo. The amusement park was opened after that. Benjamin had drawn up the plans during the dead of winter with the girls leaning over his shoulders as he sat at the dining room table penciling in the ponds, the bird cages, the souvenir stands. They liked to look at the side of his face when he was working. That face was different from the one he wore when he was preaching.

Benjamin believed that heaven would have an amusement park, that even some day if the neighbors stopped liking the idea of a religious sect living next door, they'd certainly enjoy some buggy rides, the caramel corn, a place to drink lemonade in the shade and listen to a big brass band, a ride around the park on a miniature train. They would dream of it all winter. They would be there with their hands out for their tickets as soon as spring came. They would see the truth of it—the life of the body.

And, it seemed, they did. The grounds overflowed with flowers. There were ponies for the children to ride, dancing for their parents.

Eden Springs. The most beautiful amusement park on Earth! Complete with a miniature train, a beer garden, games, a zoo, a baseball diamond, and music every night!

Cora went back to her chair and sat down.

She was so tired.

Through the open window, she could hear music starting up over at the amphitheater, a rehearsal of some kind. The musicians didn't know their parts yet, and it wasn't really music now and sounded instead as if sharp knives had been strung in the trees, wind and knives—the music of knives slicing cleanly away at a breeze—but Cora was too tired to rise from her chair and close the window.

IN THE AVIARY, ALL MANNER OF EXOTIC BIRDS:

Love birds, finches, mockingbirds, Mandarin ducks, Japanese thrushes, menagerie of animals in the little zoo.

Wallaby, kangaroo, brown bear—mother and cubs.

A mineral spring, a fish pond, a small lake stocked with shimmering fish.

If you are looking for a Paradise on earth, Eden Springs is it!

(Advertisement)

"Peacock," Eden Springs Zoo, House of David.

*B*enjamin Purnell had been his mother's twelfth child and the last thing she wanted as she lay beside his father in the cold bed between the threadbare sheets, the room full of the others sleeping, sucking, sniffling in the dark—the dark that smelled like their children's hair, milk, and bitterroot.

It was November, the end of a century, and the sky above Kentucky was cobalt and black, stuck all over with stars, some of them rising, some falling—a whole world spinning out of the universe, dropping into space without a sound.

It always filled her with despair, the falling star. The swift arc of light you almost didn't see. The utter silence as the brightness dropped behind the hills as if it had never been. She knew she'd die of it, finally, not another child, but she was moving against the man beside her in the dark anyway. The fire had already burnt down to a few glowing splinters contained in a black roundness the size of a heart—orange, then yellow, then purple, then red.

Shhh, she whispered, taking him into her, the half-sleeping man, and bit the gray flannel of his sleeve to keep from making a noise.

His whiskers on her neck. The sound of his lungs, which had always been weak, wheezing as his breath grew deeper.

And then it surprised her again, the simple pleasure. Eleven children, and never a day with enough to eat, never a night with enough rest, never a week without someone so sick that the room they all slept in together wasn't thick with the humidity of it, the gasping painful rattling.

She was forty-one with only sixteen teeth in her mouth. But not so long ago, in another life, she'd been the prettiest girl in Fleming County:

Reddish-brown hair she wore in braids, pink cheeks, blue eyes. Tiny white hands. A rosebud pout.

But the girl's face had caved in on itself as she aged. Knuckles swollen in knots big as sparrow's eggs. She'd forgotten, years before, about flirting, about laughter. She never hummed. She knew work and pain, and although she wished she didn't, because it was what forced her from day to day through the work and the pain, she knew love:

Those children with their dirty faces, their bruises and scrapes, the smells and the sounds and weight of them.

And this.

The man's flesh against hers, her flesh against the man's, the mingled pleasure, the wild quiet, the ruined body renewed.

EDEN SPRINGS

If you choose Sunday for your visit, don't think it necessary to take along the long face and somber manner usually associated with a religious sect and the Sabbath; these are indeed bright followers of Christ, and Sunday is a bright day at Eden Springs. Here in the course of the year thousands of happy and interested picnickers flock.

(Advertisement)

"*R*uth Bamford, are you in love with Benjamin Purnell?" Lena asked.

"Lena McFarlane, I have work to do."

"Picking daisies is work?"

"I have been asked to decorate the dinner table."

"Is it true he bought you a flute?"

"I have long had an interest in learning to play the flute."

"I have long had an interest in learning to play the flute."

"Lena, don't you have anything better to do? Why don't you go back in and help with the cookin'?"

"You ain't the first girl who got promised music lessons while he was hoisting up her skirts, Ruth Bamford."

No answer.

"There's someone you won't be seein' around here anymore."

No answer.

"Struck by lightning," Lena said and snorted. "Elsie Hoover. Struck by lightning in the middle of the orchard on a perfectly sunny day. Imagine that!"

"I don't know what you're trying to say, Lena, but whatever it is, I don't have the time to listen to your filth and gossip today."

"Elsie Hoover, you can't be fool enough to think he has a special desire for you?"

"I'm not listening to you, Lena."

"Do you think he means to marry you, Elsie? With all the girls here to choose from, and two or three bearing his children, and Cora Moon making all the decisions for him . . . ? You can't believe he meant it when he said you were his favorite, can you? You think that red hair of yours is really so special?"

Lena went outside and sat down on the front stoop beneath the whispering wisteria. That wisteria, it was creeping all over everything by late spring. It seemed like something preening, like a beauty that knew all about itself. If the wisteria could talk, she thought, it would talk in a nasty, dainty, little whisper, like a girl pretending to be intimate (*with you, just you*) while other people were listening.

It would like to strangle you with that pretty whisper.

Lena pulled her skirt up and looked at her stocking feet. Only the soles were dirty.

Inside the white cotton stockings, she could see her toes, the pretty arching of those.

It would take an hour to walk into town, but it would be faster and better without shoes.

Yes, she would go to town.

To town!

Without permission, without a chaperone, without telling a soul.

She would go to town and tell them what she knew.

They would listen to her.

Without shoes, if she wanted to run on her way into town, she could.

There are many other believers in the house on Superior Street. There is one young woman whose red hair hangs down her back like a curtain of flame . . .

(*The Detroit News*)

Picking fruit is not like other chores. It's full of surprises. There are pears hiding, sometimes, where you least expect to find them—near the trunk of the tree, buried deep in a nest of leaves. Sometimes you find a few cherries that have grown so close together they're just one cherry—a strange new fruit, something heavy with red that's grown a single body of skin and blood around their white stones.

But sometimes the surprise is bad. A peach that gushes in your hand when you touch it. It's too early to be overripe. Turn it in your palm, and you find what looks like a spray of bullet holes on the backside.

Worms and rot in the pink-red flesh.

It smells as if spring has been festering in it for weeks.

It was Benjamin who taught us the trick to picking apples:

The stems cannot be pulled out; they must be snapped off clean. Otherwise, where the skin is broken, the fruit will rot.

Also, apples—like all pieces of fruit—must be handled gently. Touch an apple with just the slightest bit of roughness, and your fingertips will leave a dark bruise behind.

And, because each cluster of leaves on an apple tree holds

the bud for all the future fruit, the same gentleness must be used when touching the trees.

The future is fragile. It has to be planned for.

"Girls," he said to us. "Like this," and he snapped the stem of an apple and held it in his palm.

His ring finger was in the cleft of it, moving around, a calm smile on his face.

The wind rustled the leaves of the trees, and the shadows of their branches danced across our dresses.

. . . the bodies of the Elect, in whom He shall be glorified; their bodies illuminated by that Spirit of Immortality, which shall cause their bodies to shine above that of the sun; their bodies, the stones, the lively and living stones of the great Immortal City.

(Benjamin Purnell)

At Eden Springs
House of David

*P*aradise?

Was that what it had been?

Every morning Cora used to wake up with her own golden hair in her face, tangled in a nest of herself.

"That's the darnedest hair, Cora," Benjamin would say. "I guess God really wanted you to stand out."

And her posture. She had always paid attention to her posture—her mother had taught her that—spine erect, chin high, chest lifted, as if she were always just getting ready to sing.

But she'd been a schoolteacher for so long, and the good posture, she supposed, just made them think she was some old lady with a broom up her back.

Except for Benjamin:

"Cora, you're like a pine tree. You're like a dancer. You're an arrow pointing to the heavens."

She'd let the juice from a peach linger on her lips, and she knew they'd be shining in the sunlight and sweet to kiss. She'd slip out of her dress and into Benjamin's bed in the middle of an afternoon. Her own flesh like a cup of cream spilled on the coverlet pleased her more than an eternity in heaven could have. Wings or harps or halos. She never forgot what her mother looked like in her coffin. The eternity of unfeeling ahead of her. The blank thing that passed over her face and took her away when she died.

No.

She never forgot what her mother had looked like dead.

What the bread looked like when it got moldy.

But his body.

Even as a child, he'd been beautiful.

As a boy—tall, with terrible blue eyes, reddish-brown hair, a smile like lightning. Women loved him. Long before they should have, they wanted his kisses, his hands, to sneak him into their beds when their husbands had gone to town. And the little girls would stare at him to such distraction in church that the preacher had to ask him to sit in the last pew.

He was thirty years younger than Cora was, and lightning in her arms and over her and coming up behind her— so full of life it could have lit up the darkness if she'd been able to bear the pleasure long enough to open her eyes.

There was the smell of pine about him. A sheath of muscle across his shoulders. There was a cleft in his lower lip. A small star burned on his right hip.

He'd come, his mother said, into the world with a

crown of bruises around his head. When they'd washed the blood from his infant body, they saw he was covered with a second skin—a powdery brightness that took days to wear away, and when it finally did, it left a cool light behind that would last all the days of his life.

And he was the twelfth of twelve.

Born in the month of resurrection.

Born in the last hour of the day.

Born between the waxing and the waning moons.

There were twenty-one letters in his full name—which divided by the trinity is seven . . . The Lamb with seven horns and seven eyes. The seven lamps of fire burning around the Lord. The seventh angel. Seven stars and messengers. The seven apocalyptic seals . . .

When he was still a child, he'd dreamt himself opening those seals, one by one. They were flimsy and golden-brilliant in his hands. Papery but blinding. As he broke each one, there was trumpeting and the screams of angels, which was a screaming like all the birds in the world burning and singing at the same time, and when he was done and the sealed book was open, the heavens groaned, then buckled, and then a rush of sea and bleeding washed over his bowed head.

On her walk to the school that morning so long ago, the morning he'd come to her as a boy, Cora had seen that dead frog in a ditch, oddly red, lying on its back, belly facing the sky, one of its long legs gone.

"I get these messages," he'd said, "about this paradise God wants me to make on Earth. I can see it. Full of temples . . . And you're there, in a white dress."

"Benjamin," she'd said. Her whole body was shaking.

Angeline Brown and those other girls of Fleming County, the ones with their white baptism robes clinging to their breasts in the Old Town Creek, those girls with their white skin and hair full of static—you might have thought they were virgins before Benjamin, but they weren't. They'd been running through the woods with boys since they'd been old enough to run.

But Cora Moon was.

The spinster schoolteacher. The one even Old Man Craycroft never bothered. And still, she might have been the one who lifted her face first.

Was she the one who locked the door to the Old Town Creek schoolhouse, the one who unbuttoned the two blouses she always wore, and took them off?

The boy was touching her, holding her nakedness to his. She heard him saying, very far away, "Does that hurt?"

And she was whimpering about how it didn't.

"There?" he asked. "Is that the place?"

No. Not yet. It wasn't.

He moved his fingers lower, until it was.

"Miss Moon," he groaned it. Or growled it. Or whispered it while he touched her. "I want you to feel good. I want you to feel this."

It was another voice.

Not the boy's.

A voice that came out of a body and entered hers.

A few days later she'd tendered her resignation to the Fleming County School Board. The day before that they'd found her in the berry patch with him, doing it again, and run them out of town and into their new lives.

Laura Kasischke

Can I be blamed for giving my spiritual life into the care of this man?

(Hilda Pritchard, convert)

Down by the tamarack he says, Do you believe?

And we say, No.

He says, Don't you want to be a pretty girl, just like you are now, forever and ever?

Sure, we say.

He says, Well you won't be if you don't believe.

Oh, yes I will.

Oh, no you won't. Without me, no more little pink cheeks. And these.

We slap his hand away.

He says, I don't think that's what you want, my sweet. That's what all you girls think. You think you'll be pretty and pink forever. But you won't. You know old Cora Moon? Once, she was as pretty as you.

Old Cora?

Yes. She was a beauty.

Well, seems like she believes, so—

No. No. She doesn't. She's not like you.

He says, I have something to offer you; you want to know what it is?

We say, I have heard what the others girls say that it is, and I do not want it.

He says, Eternity is a long time to be alone, but if you let me . . .

We say, Thank you very much, Mr. Purnell; I would prefer to be alone.

He says, You know you are the first girl to refuse me? What would your parents say? They, who have given up everything to bring you here to Paradise to lie with me?

They did not bring me here to lie with you, we say, and laugh out loud, right in his face.

Yes, they did. They understand. May I kiss you?

We don't say anything. We keep our eyes wide open and look around. We listen. He's found us out here alone, listening to the hum in the distance, and now . . .

There are bees in a nearby barn.

They keep bees here for the orchards, and we are not just saying this to get away from him:

We want to see those bees.

Back home, we were a meatpacking people, but not anymore. No more blood curdling in barrels in the summer heat. No more stringy-muscled sheep laid out for stripping on the lawn. Our parents have brought us here because the world is going to end, and being here will save us.

A whole barn full of bees is over there droning in the daylight, in the dark of that hive. We push him away, and we say, Show me them bees.

He looks up smiling from the buttons of our blouses. Now he's happy. There's a bulge in his pants, and his neck is red, but he knows now that we are asking about bees instead of trying to get away, that he's going to have us after all, so he can wait, so we button ourselves back up, and we walk across the orchard to the barn, and he shows us how to cup our hands

Eden Springs
(69)

to a crack in the wall, and he says, See? He says, You have to have bees—for the orchard. What's an orchard without bees to set the fruit, to pollinate the flowers? Without bees, you have nothing.

All that breathing. He never just says a thing; he breathes it.

But, with our hands cupped to that crack, we can see:

Long, dripping combs fastened to the ceiling and the walls and the floors with wax. Arches and pillars of honey, glowing, even in the darkness and the shadows.

Glowing. Buzzing. Golden. Dangerous and sweet.

And, in the center of it, a dark clot that rises and falls and rises.

Like some kind of heart.

Like some piece of secret.

He's running his hands over our bodies, and all that breathing. He's got his face in our long hair, and finally we sigh. We turn to him, and say, Go ahead and do what you want to do to me.

It's not only for me, you know, my beautiful, fumbling with the buttons.

That's what they said you'd say, we say.

Josie Lewis came running down the stairs like someone scared to death and I asked her what was the matter, she said Benjamin met her in the upper balcony, and grabbed her in a room and closed the door after her.

(Mildred Giles, deposition)

"*Feel that, angel?*" *he whispered.* "*That's eternal life.*"

Ruth Bamford laughed. She said, "I feel that. That's a man pushin' around up inside my skirts."

He laughed, too.

He always said, "You know, you are the only girl around here complaining about me."

And she said, "No, I'm not. I'm just the only one complainin' to your face."

He said, "I like that. You're a fighter. I like a girl who speaks her mind. Feel that?"

She let him, but later when he said, "Now let us bow our heads and pray," at the dinner table, she just stared straight ahead, stared straight at him.

"You're a sullen one."

She stared him straight in the eye and said, "I want a flute."

"Well," Benjamin said, "I'll buy you a flute if that's really what you want. But you know the other girls'll get jealous. They might take the ax to your flute."

"And," she said, "I don't want to pick fruit no more. I'm sick of pickin'. I want a job at the amusement park. I want to be a ticket taker."

He cleared his voice. It was like a laugh. She narrowed her eyes. She was also tired of listening to him laugh.

"That would be just fine except that you are such a scowler. I don't know that folks coming to Eden Springs for a happy outing will appreciate having their tickets taken by a girl as surly as you."

"Get me the flute," Ruth Bamford said. "I have," she said, "an interest in learnin' to play the flute."

A few days later, she had it.

The flute was shiny, and it seemed brand new, but when she tried to play it, she felt as if something was scraping its way all along her nerves. Something bright and made of metal.

It hurt her teeth.

Twice or three times, she smacked that flute against the plaster wall of her room but only dented it.

A few questions I cannot answer: Why is Miss M. H. losing her reason? Why was Miss P. P. hurried back to England mentally unbalanced? Why are Miss E. J. and E. M. and a few others kept in silk dresses . . . ? Why was Mrs. E. C. presented with a silver trombone horn when she could not play a note? She was often seen hanging about the halls upstairs.

(Harry Williams, *Mysteries, Errors and Injustices at House of David*, pamphlet)

"*Elsie,*" he said, "*you ought to start sewing a quilt for your bridal bed.*"

Elsie Hoover turned around fast at the oven with a peach pie on a tin plate held out in her hands. The pie was warm, and the smell of it was fruit and burning. The others were in the kitchen, too, cleaning up the supper things, making tea.

"My bridal bed?" she asked. And saying the words *bridal* and *bed* together made her blush.

Benjamin laughed. He said, "Slice me a piece of that pie, my beauty." He was leaning against the doorjamb, moving all over her with sleepy eyes, and then he went back to the dining room to wait.

When Elsie turned to the counter with the pie, to slice it, the girls were staring at her. Surely she'd simply slipped on the dusty hem of her long skirt, she thought when she opened her eyes again and found herself staring up at a circle of them staring down at her.

But the pie was splattered all over everything, and there was blood at her temple, and Elsie thought she remembered something coming from behind her, shoving her hard before she fell forward and hit her head on the heavy oak table and it all went black.

"Oh, poor Elsie," Myrtle, the pregnant girl, said.

"Oh, darlin', let me help you up," another one said and offered her a little white hand.

Part Three

Benjamin talked to us and told us he was just like Jesus and had the
right to have intercourse with us girls.

(Lena McFarlane, affidavit)

ISRAELITE COLONY VIEW
Benton Harbor, Mich., U.S.A.
Send for literature.

*T*he way Ruth Bamford had long had an interest in playin' the flute, Lena McFarlane had long had a daydream about a dress:

It was a green satin dress with a row of pearl buttons down the back that stretched clear from the nape of the neck to the hem.

In her daydream, she wore this dress with a broad-brimmed hat and, carrying a parasol, wandered about Eden Springs on the arm of Will Williams (a boy from town who had washed the windows of the Diamond House once, a boy she'd walked straight up to and introduced herself to on account of his big smile and strong-looking arms). In her daydream, she let Will Williams buy her a sugar cone, and she ate it neatly, dabbing at her mouth with a square lace hankie, laughing loudly at something Will Williams said.

"Shall we take a stroll down by the duck pond?" she'd ask, and he'd say yes. No one from the Colony would have recognized her yet.

Lena and Will Williams would walk a ways together, her in that satin dress and him in a nice pair of black pants and a clean white shirt, and then she'd see Myrtle Sassman or Estelle Kits or Elizabeth Stroupe looking at her from behind the ticket counter where they'd been standing on their sore feet all day, or looking up at her from their hands and knees in the roses where they were plucking weeds.

"By gosh. Lena. Is that you?"

Lena would turn in her daydream then and smile and say, "Yes, it is. Why, I didn't even notice you there!"

"Lena McFarlane. Where have you been all these years?"

"Oh, didn't you know? I'm Mrs. Will Williams now. I moved to town, and now Will and I are living in a house in St. Joe. I'd like you to meet my husband Mr. Williams. He now owns the Whitcomb Hotel."

And just as Will Williams was bowing to the girls, who were gaping at him with their mouths open, Benjamin would appear from behind the shadow of a leafy tree. He'd catch his breath when he saw Lena, put his hand to his heart. All that green satin. And her hair (maybe it was bobbed) in wisps around her face beneath the broad-brimmed hat.

"By God," Benjamin would say in a choked hush. "It's Lena McFarlane."

He'd see that she was a lady then.

Laura Kasischke

Maybe he'd wish he was her father then.

(There were plenty of people who said he was her father. Lena knew that. But she also knew he wasn't. She knew that Brother Macintyre was her father. She could tell by the way he stared at her in the chapel with eyes just like the ones she saw when she passed her own reflection in the mirror. Fatherlike, and very sad.)

Maybe he'd wish he was her lover or her husband, or simply that all along he'd taken more notice of her. He'd wish he'd bought her a flute instead of Ruth Bamford and that he'd made sure that Otto Kepler had given her lessons on how to play it.

Then he'd be a happy man.

Now he knew that, but now it was too late.

This is the daydream Lena McFarlane dreamed, as she so often did, as she walked the two miles down the dusty road in her stocking feet into town, while the sky glittered over her like the inside of something—a smashed-open jewel, a daydream—and the sweetness of blossom time was in the air.

In the gardens and along the road were mostly peonies and daisies, but Lena's favorite flower was the poppy, and when she passed a clapboard house on the way into town that had a wall of them around it, she stopped and stared. She watched them dance in the breeze. Or squirm. Their faces were on fire. Their tongues were black. All that heat and brilliance, swimming.

An old lady peered out at her from behind a lace curtain, and Lena lifted her hand to wave, but the old lady disappeared before Lena had time.

Then wagon wheels crunched behind her, and Lena turned around.

"Hello there."

It was the police wagon, and Constable Schmidt was driving it. His dappled horse was wearing blinders, nodding as if to some secret tune.

"Would you like a ride into town?" the Constable called out, and Lena said, "Oh, yes, sir, thank you," and hurried over.

He reached out a thick and hairy hand to help her up, slapped the reins, and the horse trotted onward, and Lena got jostled into the Constable's shoulder, and then she put her hands in her lap and stared straight ahead.

They didn't speak.

There was so much to see.

A billboard for shaving cream. A woman wearing a striped skirt carrying a loaf of bread. A man who was either very drunk or sleeping on a bench beneath a lamppost, mouth open.

The road billowed up in front of them as a cloud of dust. The horse simply trotted through it, and it parted for him, swirling away. But Lena could taste that dust on her teeth. The road was in her nose, on her lips. People stared at them from the street corners, and she thought she heard music coming from inside a place with a sign outside that said "Stu's Tavern" on the door.

She might go back to the Colony some day, she thought, but when she did, by God, she would be wearing that green satin dress, and she would be bringing this world back with her.

(Bessie) Woodworth recounted how, by the age of fifteen, Benjamin was using her for his pleasure . . . According to her, Benjamin was preparing her body for the Millennium.

(Clare E. Adkins, *Brother Benjamin*)

*T*here he was again, smelling his way up to 'Elsie Hoover's room. Following all that pale red hair that fanned around her, scented with air.

She was a tiny girl for sixteen. Like the weak rose on a bush of roses. Prettier, but sickly.

Myrtle had heard him say to her the other day, "Elsie, you ought to start sewing a quilt for your bridal bed," as he leaned so casually in the kitchen doorway, talking to Elsie as if no else could hear, and Myrtle had wanted to cry out, "And what about your big fat wife Queen Mary in all her fancy dresses?"

Queen Mary, Benjamin's "wife," had just wandered through the house again in one of her green satin gowns, playing deaf and dumb or muttering to God.

"And what about all these other girls and their passage into Paradise?"

"And what about Myrtle Sassman, seven months with child?"

Instead, Myrtle had bitten her lip, hard, tasting blood, and thought of the first time she'd seen him, standing out there behind her father's barn.

She had been gathering eggs that day.

How she'd hated gathering eggs!

Dull and dangerous at the same time. All those eggs in the pockets of her aprons. Featherless and faceless, and each one with that yellow fire inside it.

And of all the girls, her, Elsie Hoover, who wouldn't even sit on his lap of an evening. Who wouldn't even look at him. Who, when it came time to pray, would be twiddling her thumbs nervously, glancing around at the other girls, who were watching her, just waiting for her to look at him.

Now Elizabeth Stroupe was sitting on a bench in the hallway between the kitchen and the stairwell, chewing a piece of her own hair and watching him climb those stairs on his way to Elsie Hoover's room.

Myrtle looked away.

Elizabeth's was a kind of suffering in which she herself did not plan, ever, to be seen:

A mourning dove with a broken wing, a rabbit caught under the wagon wheel.

They were everywhere around the Colony, and he couldn't bear it—suffering—and yet, he wouldn't put them out of their misery himself. Instead, he'd run after one of the boys who was used to that sort of thing, tell him what to do, tell the boy that the best way to kill a sick or injured kitten was to take a hammer to the back of its head, as if he had ever done it himself. Benjamin would be far away before the boy got back with a hammer. Whimpering things, helpless things, he hated these even more than he hated these things dead.

"He's going to marry her, too, I hear," Elizabeth Stroupe said to Myrtle from her bench. "I heard him telling her.

Begging her. He said he's going to make her the Bride of Christ. The New Queen of Eden. He said—"

"He's got a wife."

"He told her it don't matter. He got a wife besides Queen Mary, too. And another one somewheres in Ohio. He told her he would only take one more before he died, and it was her, because she was the prettiest, and she was the best, and she—"

Myrtle Sassman couldn't stand it. She crossed the hallway and raised her hand, and before she realized that she was the one who'd done it, Elizabeth Stroupe's sweet, bitter little face had been slapped.

Regarding the so-called "Purification rites," when, where, and how it happened to me, I will tell you. I was walking through the hall at Shiloh, when I heard Benjamin call my name. He stood before the open door of his room which he told me to enter . . .

(Hilda Pritchard, *The Truth about the House of David*)

Mourning doves—those pearly-soft pairs swarmed all over Eden Springs. Their cooing, to us, was morning, nothing sad about it, the mild pink-gray light of dawn. We liked to watch them mate in the forsythia—the female fluttering her wings in muffled silence, the male shimmering pink above her, winging as though any moment he might be ready to fly, taking her with him.

It was ecstasy, blurred, going nowhere.

"They're pretty birds," Benjamin said when we admired them aloud.

"They mate for life," we told him, and maybe when we said it, our voices trembled.

"Sure, my lovelies," he said, chuckling. "They mate for life, but they don't love."

He put his arms around our waists then and let his hand drift like a thought across our hips.

The Widders Family: "After Mabel's death her father went insane and the burden of his cries was concerning the daughter and the way she had been wronged. He got so bad that they tied him to a tree in the orchard and when the girls passed back and forth he took on terrible. The mother went insane and was sent to the asylum at Kalamazoo."

(Attorney General's records, State Records Center, Lansing, Michigan)

*I*t was a large, strange room. *Nearly empty, and echoing,* and the men all pulled up wooden chairs that shrieked across the wooden floors, and they straddled them backwards and inched in on her, and one of them had a pad of paper, and the others were chewing pencils and toothpicks.

Their faces were full of excitement.

Lena had never had an audience before.

This was what it was: an audience.

Lena took a deep breath, and the men seemed to hover on that breath and lean in even closer, and they didn't even blink when she opened her mouth to speak:

"I heard one of the girls say, *It was one thing when it was all of us, but if he's thinkin' Elsie Hoover is going to be the New Queen of Eden, that's another thing.*"

The men didn't take their eyes off her. They all started nodding at once. One of them with a yellow pad of paper said, "And did you hear them making threats against the life of this girl?"

Another one, with a mustache and a blue hat, said, "Yes. Did you hear them making any threats?" as if maybe she hadn't already heard the question right the first time.

"Well," Lena said and even managed to laugh. "I saw one girl with a length of rope. That seemed like a threat to me."

She held her hands apart about the size of the rope she'd seen Elizabeth Stroupe carrying across the lawn.

"And I saw the others with their baskets, wearing their orchard hats, heading out the door a few minutes behind Elsie, who'd been told there was some work for her out there and that she should go to the far end of the cherry orchard and that they would all come out and meet her there."

There was a long pause as the one man wrote and the other men whispered and another one ran off to fetch her a glass of water, as if she were the Queen. There was sun on the floor and on her arms. It was just warm enough. Lena took the cool glass of water from the man, who bowed when he handed it to her, and she looked out the dirty window of the sheriff's office, and saw a cart go by:

KNIVES SHARPENED! SCISSORS! RAZORS! ALL EDGES AND BLADES!

The grinder was driving it.

Rupert Kepler.

He'd been, himself, a member of the House of David for a while, Rupert Kepler. He'd left when he'd found his wife with Benjamin, kissing him in the parlor of the Diamond House. He'd run in to find her and to tell her that their only boy was sick with pneumonia and wanted his mama, whom he had not seen since she had been relocated from the cottage in which they'd been living, as grinders and caretakers at Eden Springs, to the bedroom next to Benjamin's.

("Rupert, you must let me tend to Marietta," Benjamin had told him. "She's weak in the faith. I'll return her to you when she's been purified and made new.")

"You're a fraud!" Rupert Kepler started yelling and screaming, shaking his fists at the Diamond House as he rode away with the boy on a Saturday morning in October.

Lena had been watching from the porch. Over her head she could hear Marietta giggling and sobbing in Benjamin's bed, and him singing some hymn to drown out Rupert Kepler's shouting.

Now the grinder's white horse nodded its head politely in Lena's direction.

It was saying, she thought, *Lena McFarlane, welcome to your new life.*

I have talked with about all of the girls in the colony and they have all
told me the same story, that they have been intimate with Benjamin
. . .

(Augusta Holliday, affidavit)

*T*he reporters found their way to the Diamond House before the police, and they stood around in their black hats on the front lawn scratching pencils across their pads. They threw cigarette butts into the lilies. Benjamin came out and stood on the porch in his white suit and answered their questions.

"The woman died on the eleventh day of May. It is our belief that the dead should be disregarded by the living."

"So you left her to rot in the orchard?"

"Yes."

"And didn't report the death?"

"No."

"So you decided to disregard the laws of the state?"

"We follow a higher law than that of the state."

"How did this woman die?"

"She died of natural causes due to a lack of natural faith."

There was some snickering among the reporters about that.

"What was her age?" someone asked.

"I am told that she was sixty-eight," Benjamin answered.

"Is that tho?" a reporter with a lisp asked.

"Yeth," Benjamin said, "thath tho."

The other reporters laughed, but that one turned red and began to stammer:

"Well, well, well—ya got one of yer own girl-th in town claimin' this one was but a thirteen-year-old and that she died in the orchard on a perfectly thunny day."

"Yeth," Benjamin nodded. "That-th what I heard, too."

Much more laughter. A dog ran across the lawn then, yapping at the reporters, jumping against Benjamin, licking its big pink tongue up to his face. Benjamin knelt down to pat the dog roughly, and the dog began to wag its tail wildly, whining with adoration.

"What's your dog's name?" a reporter called out.

"My dog's name is Dice," Benjamin said, looking up from the dog, which he had never seen before. "I got another dog, also named Dice."

"Why's that?" the reporter asked.

"So that I've got me a Paradise," Benjamin said, and as they laughed he tipped his white hat to the reporters, turned his back, went into the Diamond House, and closed the door behind him.

Women's faces betray them. When I visited the House of David I saw no hard-faced women. I saw women whose faces betrayed simplicity and innocence . . . I do not believe King Ben to be guilty.

(Governor Chase S. Osborn)

There was a tamarack grew down by the well. In the summer its branches grew so heavy with leaves they would bend all the way to the ground. The shade there was thick, and it smelled always of dew—that cool smell of water rising from the ground, the earth's wet breath, the fresh mineral springs under everything.

One evening after dinner, he found us there, he took our hand in his, and we sat together in the tent of shadow that tamarack made. It was nearly dusk, and there were fireflies starting to blink near the top of the tree, which looked like a dark skeleton from where we were.

A skull full of stars.

As it got darker, there were more stars and more darkness, and the fireflies flitted away.

But Benjamin's eyes were bright, and his hair smelled like pine. He had all that long hair, and those dark, deep eyes. His face, chiseled from stone, and his body—

He eased us backward in the cool grass, pushed up our skirts. He undid the buttons of our white blouse, took off his own shirt, and we touched the muscles on his chest, the coarse hair there, pressed into the salt smell of it, and we became one thing, writhing and moaning naked near the well, the bones of our hips clapping into his, straining, entwined, his tongue in our mouth, and his breath inside our body.

We'd waited a long time for this.

And it was just as the others had said it would be.

Laura Kasischke

It will be said of them, in heaven they have been.

(Benjamin Purnell)

"*B*enjamin," *Cora said when he came in, closing the* door behind him, "you have to marry these girls off. There will be trouble. Elsie Hoover is just the beginning of this trouble. Or she could be the end of it. This trouble could be the end of everything."

"Marry them off?" Benjamin asked.

The strange wild dog was on the other side of the door, scratching at it. Cora got up and pounded on it to scare the dog away.

"Marry my girls off?"

A boy again.

There it was.

The boy in the schoolhouse. That boy was still there, just as he had always been.

"Yes, Benjamin," Cora said. "There's bound to be an investigation, and this many unmarried girls, and some of them in the family way—it will not hold up to their suspicions. Benjamin? Will it?"

Benjamin stood looking at his white shoes for a very long time, and then he shook his head, and then he nodded, considering a loose thread on the sleeve of his white suit as if it held some secret message. Outside, there were photographers aiming their cameras at the Diamond House, bright bursts of flashbulb, reporters tossing their cigarette butts into the lilies.

"Get them married, Benjamin. Before the week is out. And, Benjamin, never touch them again. You've got to keep your hands off the girls, or everything we—"

He was shaking his head again, as if refusing to hear or shaking something loose.

"Benjamin," Cora said, louder this time, like the schoolteacher she had been before him. "You must have nothing more to do with the girls. The state has been waiting for this," she said. "The world has been waiting for this."

Benjamin cleared his throat, as if he were about to address a crowd, and this time he nodded, obediently—but when he finally spoke, it was just a muffled mutter.

The Fleming Family: "Came from New Zealand, Malcom Fleming, wife, and daughter. They brought some property, money, and stock. The daughter lived in Jerusalem House, and it is uncertain as to whether Benjamin had anything to do with her. The girl went insane and made certain outcries or charges against Benjamin and she was sent to Kalamazoo; later was sent to New Zealand, where she is now in an asylum."

(Attorney General's records, Nichol's trial notes)

*P*aul *Kleinchnecht, Rufus Hanaford, Frank Rogers,* Leonard Rowe, Sam Smiley, Hix Vaughn, Marcus Tyler, Dwight Baushke, Leonard Baushke, Henry Baushke, David Baushke, Andrew Bell, Glen Crow, Charles Caudle, Fred Cady, Carl Tucker, Virgil Smith, Henry Stroupe, Martin Swant, Owen Swant, Preston Williams, Austin Williams, Hugh Walker, Frank Wylands, Herbert Vogler, Cletis Wade, Tiflis Walstrom, Gustaf Walstrom . . .

The names were written out in Benjamin's hand, the splotches and slashes he used for commas and to dot his *i*'s when he was in a hurry.

There were twenty-seven names for the twenty-seven girls.

When the piece of paper was handed to Myrtle, she stared at it. Those names blurred together as she tried to remember the men whose names those were:

Names spilled all over the floor like batter, impossible to scoop back up.

Soft sloppy names. Vowels like yawns.

The Baushke brothers with their identical bulbous

noses. Gustav Walstrom, who was just a skinny boy with a club foot. Cletis Wade, on the other hand, was a fat old man she'd talked to once about taxidermy. He'd been a taxidermist before coming to the House of David, and now he regretted all that death. And Fred Cady had buck teeth. Preston and Austin Williams both had lisps.

One of them for each of the girls.

Elizabeth Stroupe was chewing on her hair, looking around the parlor from inside that hair like a squirrel making itself a nest out of its own fur.

Elizabeth Stroupe might as well be dead.

It had been a week since Elsie Hoover had been found in the orchard.

"Girls," Old Cora said, "I'm sure you understand the importance of this. Benjamin says here—" and she read it again, the part about the state of Michigan, the tampering, and no girl staying at the Colony unless she'd chosen the name of one of these men off the list and was prepared to marry him.

Myrtle thought again of the first time she'd seen Benjamin standing behind her father's barn, as if it were some bit of ribbon that had got stuck in a branch, blowing over and over and over again around her face.

All those eggs in her pockets. Each one with that yellow fire inside it.

"Benjamin said to have you girls dropped off at the Printing Shop now. It's been fixed up. Bedrooms and bathrooms and all. There's no rooms left in the Diamond House, and we're trying to get the parlor set up for the wedding."

His people reverence him. Their love and loyalty are patent. Although a despot, he must have been a kindly monarch.

(Judge Fead's opinion)

He says, "You have to have bees, my beauties—for the orchard. What's an orchard without bees to set the fruit, to pollinate the flowers? Without bees, you have nothing, my cuties."

. . . They shall ascend with Christ into heaven, where, because of their perfect bodies, they shall sit nearest to the heavenly throne and be greater than the angels even . . .

(Benjamin Purnell, *The Book of Wisdom*)

*P*aul *Kleinchnecht.*

Myrtle Sassman picked him off the list because he was the first one on it, and none of the other girls would pick, and finally Cora Moon handed the list to her and said, "You're the one who's got to go first, since you're the one they aren't going to need to examine to know there's been tampering."

Myrtle picked up the pencil and wrote her initials, M. S., next to his name.

No.

Myrtle Kleinchnecht. It was an awful name. She tried to snatch the paper back, but Cora Moon had already passed it on, and she gave Myrtle a look to let her know there would be no taking it back.

Paul Kleinchnecht?

No.

All Myrtle remembered about him was that he had, perhaps, a strong singing voice.

A tenor.

If she was not mistaken, she believed she'd heard him sing with the jazz band the summer before. He'd been clicking his fingers and tapping his foot as he sang, and she'd been vaguely impressed by his cheerfulness, his tunefulness—although she'd had no desire to marry them.

When Elizabeth Stroupe finally managed to take the hair out of her mouth, she simply sat huddled in the corner, holding her knees in her arms, rocking back and forth, sobbing, until Old Cora grabbed her arm hard in her hand and yanked her to her feet and said, "We've got one man left, and unless you take him you're going to be sent away, and then what will you do?"

Elizabeth didn't say a word.

Cora Moon wrote her initials, E. S., next to Hix Vaughn's name.

All denominations teach salvation of the soul. The higher glory we are striving for is life of the body without death.

(T. Dewhirst, convert)

*I*t was raining when the wedding carriages pulled up to the Printing Shop a few days later—four buggies pulled by workhorses, driven by old men.

We were all in white.

But we had always been all in white.

Some of the gowns were frayed and dirty around the hems, worn before by girls too short for the length of them.

One of the buggies was driven by Elizabeth Stroupe's father, and all the way to the Diamond House all he talked about was Elizabeth, how the pesticides had turned her hair white, eaten straight through her stomach. She'd been standing up stiff as a rake in the shed when they found her two days before. And who would have thought that a poison intended to kill a worm but spare a peach could eat straight through the stomach of a girl?

Stroupe had to stop crying long enough to stop the buggy in the rain, to get a knot out of the horse's reins—and the horse, a big dark draft horse, was shivering with flies, even in the rain, its back rippling like a wet old rug as it shivered.

Flies on its back, under its tail, trotting casually over its open eyes.

Q. Do you remember any of the girls—Mary Estes, Elizabeth Stroupe, Violet Boruff, Rosie Boruff, Maggie Vieritz, Jewell Boone, Ola Boone, Jane Perrenoud, Helen Perrenoud, Carrie Rein, Dolly Wheeler, Bessie Daniels, Countess Drake, Tiflis Drake, Eva Lane and Grace Lane—you knew all those girls, didn't you, Mr. Purnell?

A. . . . I don't remember those girls . . .

(The testimony of Benjamin Purnell given in open court

in the trial of the *State of Michigan v. the House of David*)

*M*yrtle couldn't see him during the ceremony because David Baushke, who was six and a half feet tall, was standing beside Sophie Fleming in front of Myrtle and Paul Kleinchnecht. She hadn't seen Benjamin since the day the reporters had come, the day Lena McFarlane had run off, and that was only as he hurried past her to his room and closed the door.

But he was close now. She knew his voice at the front of the room. He was mumbling something about love and faith and a good wife being darn near as good as a loyal horse—at which the new grooms chuckled all at once with a sound like ducks running quickly across muck—and then he was gone, before she'd even glimpsed his white hat, the beard, the hands, the hair.

Violet Boruff wept sloppily into her hands as her new husband signed some papers, tongue stuck out as he tried to remember how to spell his new bride's maiden name, and afterward, they ate some cake.

Ten cakes had been made for the reception, but four of them had collapsed before they left the oven, so the couples ate only small slivers, politely, of what there was. A few of the brides offered Myrtle their pieces of cake because she looked so big and starved, but she declined.

She had no taste for cake. One small slice was plenty.

And the room was too crowded.

She could hardly breathe. The smell of all those working men in it. A faint tang of dirty water splashed onto rotting wood. It was the same room where they'd danced night after winter night—with each other, with Benjamin. His Hawaiian music on the phonograph. That steel music—the scratching of a needle over black and spinning plastic, the miracle of the music of an island on the other side of the world—a dot in an ocean under a balmy sky—funneled into the Diamond House parlor through a tube on a winter night. Nothing but frozen Michigan trees out there—but inside the Diamond House, Benjamin turned water into wine, and they drank it and danced with Benjamin, who wore no shoes.

When the whole thing was over, Paul Kleinchnecht said goodnight politely. The rain had ended, and the sky had cleared, and he walked her halfway back to the Printing Shop without speaking until they parted.

"'Night, Myrtle."

Myrtle looked at him closely in the moonlight for the first time and noticed that he had only one long eyebrow and that it seemed to stretch from one of his temples to the other.

Estelle Kits and Violet Boruff and some of the others had started crying just before the cake, and their sobs were ragged and very wet, and they continued to cry long after all the brides had taken off their white dresses, put on their nightgowns, and gotten into their cots.

"Shut up," someone finally snapped in the darkness, and the crying stopped, and in the silence Myrtle thought she heard a cat hiss viciously outside. Someone said, "Some of these husbands are plenty handsome. We should ——"

"They're not Benjamin Purnell."

Another one said, "For God's sake, be quiet."

Over to one side of this cemetery is a stretch of gravelly sand, with an occasional sprig of stunted grass. Here about fifty of the House of David cult are buried.

(*The New York Times*, April 29, 1923)

*H*e hurried away from the cemetery and tossed his shovel into the shed and vowed to think no more about it—but that night the gravedigger had a bad dream.

And the next and the next.

The first part of the dream was just the way it had been, the way they'd come to town. One by one.

"They're good folks," his father used to say, "like us. They're Christians. Hard workers. We don't own this town. They have a right to their House of David."

But his mother and most of the others didn't like it at all. No one was flattered at first to find out that God had told Benjamin Purnell to build an Eden in Benton Harbor, to call it the House of David, to call all of God's people to it to prepare for the Judgment Day.

Mostly, the people of Benton Harbor were fruit farmers. Peaches, apples, cherries—freestone and cling. Only Main Street was paved.

It seemed, at best, like some kind of a mistake.

He and his mother saw Benjamin for the first time in the open market. It was summer, and she whispered harsh and loud as they passed, "Don't look at that heathen."

But it was too late.

He'd looked at Benjamin Purnell, and Benjamin Purnell had looked at him and smiled. Amused. He'd lowered his eyebrows, teasing. He'd heard her:

Heathen.

All that hair.

It was neatly brushed down his back, as long as any woman's, and he was wearing a pure white suit. Who wore a white suit in Benton Harbor? And it wasn't the least bit dirty.

In a second, Benjamin Purnell was gone, and his mother reached down and slapped him on the side of the head.

Not hard, but it made him itch and cry.

In the dream, it was the beginning:

King Ben in a white suit and then a few women in white dresses and then a dozen men with long hair, like his, laughing at the train station. And then everywhere, they'd be there, where before there'd only been the same farmers and store-people for all those years. Suddenly—in the bank, in the bakery, in the Dry Goods Store.

Soon there were as many of these new strangers as there'd ever been of anyone else.

And then the amusement park, the miniature train. People came from far away to see these things. The baseball team got famous. They could beat any other team in the minor leagues and draw a crowd with their long hair and strangeness.

Bands, ice cream, a beer garden, a bird house, an exotic-animal zoo. They built a hotel for the tourists—and another and another. Street after street was cobbled or paved. Year after year, they came. New converts. From Europe. Australia. New accents and foreign languages every day. They looked happy. They planned, it seemed, to stay.

A gravedigger (which his father also was) sees a growing population as a good and necessary thing.

Mostly they were young, but there are always diseases and eventually age.

A gravedigger can wait. Although, there were jokes: "Nobody's gonna need your services around here anymore! Not with King Ben. Didn't ya hear, we're all gonna live forever. You might as well give your shovel away."

"We'll see about that," his father would say. "If nobody dies, I'll trade it in for a rake."

Even his mother started to like them.

"Really," she said, "the nicest manners."

Benjamin Purnell learned her name, and more than once she blushed when he winked at her in the market.

In June, they'd go down to Eden Springs when it opened for the first day of summer, and his parents would listen to the band while he rode around and around on the train.

And that's how it started in the dream—with a feeling of pleasure, seeing these people with their long hair, in their white clothes, always polite and smiling. He'd be watching the girls in their starched dresses, listening to the music and smelling the sweetness of the lilies, and seeing King Ben strolling among them and the sky bright blue.

Then he'd get a funny feeling:

Maybe the sky was a bit too blue. Maybe the music

in the band shell had gotten louder. Something about it sounded wrong, sounded like a dirge instead of a polka—trumpets and wailing, and a low, deep marching drum—and then he'd notice that one of those girls, one with loose strawberry-colored braids and parted lips and blue-gray eyes, was looking at him from across the duck pond. Laughing, fanning herself with a piece of plain paper.

In the dream, he staggered backwards and started to scream, seeing her there, out of the grave he'd buried her in, out of the earth and alive. The way she turned right at him and smiled made him wake up cold and soaked in sweat and clawing at the blankets to stumble out of bed night after night, until finally he was relieved instead of surprised when the sheriff came by to tell him that a girl from the Colony claimed that the box he'd buried a couple weeks before had not contained the remains of a sixty-eight year old woman, dead of apoplexy, after all, but those of a sixteen-year-old girl who'd been choked to death in the orchard, and that the state was asking him to dig her up again.

Sometimes he read sacred writings to us in the evening and sometimes he read dirty stories and laughed like a madman.

(Estelle Mills, convert)

*P*aul Baushke stood on the porch with his hands stuffed in his pockets, and when Cora Moon stepped out, he wouldn't look at her.

"Did you put the pesticides in the garden shed, Paul?"

He nodded.

"You know how to build a coffin, don't you, Paul?"

"Course, ma'am."

"And you got the wagon set to go?"

"Yes, ma'am."

"And you know how to dig a grave and bury a box and take another box away?"

He nodded.

"And you've got your brothers set to help you if it's too much for you?"

"Yes."

"Good, then. Don't go telling anybody anything, and don't be a fool. Come look for me in the garden shed to-night around twelve o'clock. I expect to be put in that box and taken to Crystal Springs and buried there. And then you put that other coffin in your wagon, and dig a hole off in the woods, beyond the orchard, and cover it over with pine needles, and nothing else."

Like a good, slow student, he nodded, and Cora Moon felt pleased with him, and touched. It seemed right that Paul Baushke would be the last student she would ever have.

That night, she took her time walking to the shed. It was a crystal-clear night. A host of constellations telling stories in the sky. She knew all those stories. She had a few of her own. She had spent, she realized, just enough nights on her back in this life, looking up to the stars. She'd had meals full of needles, and others so sweet she could barely stand to think of herself eating them. Bowls full of fruit like pure sweetness dropped out of the sky, and she remembered Benjamin telling a crowd of women and men with long hair standing in the twilight of a June evening in the orchard, "Someday people will point and say, `That's where the House of David was.' Some day people will have forgotten all about us."

It had seemed impossible.

Imagining that day, when they would be gone, replaced by nothing, an old story, some lost curiosity—

It was a still night. The stars did not even twinkle. But there had been a stiff breeze that other evening, and Benjamin's white hat had blown off his head, and it went rolling across the green grass, and there was chaos and laughter as the children chased after the tumbling brightness into the dying day.

Hatless in the breeze, Benjamin had done a little dance to entertain the crowd full of believers and nonbelievers who wanted to believe, until some boy brought it back, and then he went on:

"Someday," he'd said, trying to regain the seriousness

he'd lost, "we will be gone. Risen. Glorified."

The sky was the color and substance—exactly the color and substance—of a slice of blueberry pie.

Cora Moon closed the door to the garden shed quietly behind her.

In the Summer of 1922, Pullen . . . was told by E. B. Martinie, an undertaker, that "another of those House of Davids had died," and the body would be sent out. It was supposed to be one of the older members of the colony, a woman of 68.

Although they claim immortality, the cult has a contract with Martinie to attend to funerals at so much a body.

Pullen said, "As I tried to lower the box, one corner broke. Anything would break it for it was thin enough to poke a finger through.

"Inside I could see the shoulders, neck and face of a girl. She was wrapped in old brown paper, like a mummy, and the paper had broken . . ."

(*The New York Times*, April 29, 1923)

HOUSE OF DAVID
BENTON HARBOR, MICHIGAN

hey came down from Lansing and Grand Rapids, dressed in suits, carrying badges. The gravedigger took them straight to the spot. It still looked fresh. It was easy to find.

"You're sure this is it?" the lead investigator asked. He was a tall man with one eye that wouldn't stay put. It wandered over the gravedigger's face, while the other eye stayed fixed to its place.

"I'm sure this is it."

The other ones—there were seven of them—all whipped out pads of paper at the same time and began looking around them and taking notes, although there was nothing to take notes about—just a stretch of gravelly sand with a sprig or two of stunted grass growing here or there.

No mounds, no tombstones. About fifty concrete posts with numbers on them.

"Then you can start digging," the leader with the loose blue eye told the gravedigger.

It was the end of June by then. A day that threatened to storm. The sky was deep purple beyond the leaves of the oaks that bordered the cemetery, and you could feel the lake, only a mile away—you could feel that it was rough and wild. It made a kind of thrumming under the ground on those rough days.

Sand is always easy to dig at the top, where it's light and dry. Deceptively easy. The state officials watched as he dug. One of them took out a cigarette and lit it, and the smell of a struck match mixed with the smell of rain and lake snaking its way through the air.

But you hit a few feet down, and the sand gets heavy. It's dense and wet, and it doesn't want to budge. The grave-digger stabbed at it with the shovel, trying to loosen it before digging more, but it wouldn't even crack. It was like slamming a shovel into concrete. He took off his shirt and tossed it behind him. The state officials watched. The one who'd smoked a cigarette lit another.

It took two hours to hit the boxwood of the coffin, and the gravedigger felt briefly that he might be sick when he did. The state officials, who were sitting under a tree now, stood up when they heard the noise.

"That's the coffin?" the leader asked.

"Yes," the gravedigger said.

They were all crowding around now, whipping out those notepads, looking into the hole at the bit of boxwood. A smell like honeysuckle rose up from it, a kind of sweetness so thick you're drinking it instead of breathing. The gravedigger had smelled it plenty, but the officials grabbed for their handkerchiefs and put them over their noses and mouths.

The gravedigger started shoveling again, tossing the dirt off the coffin, panting, until he'd cleared the whole top off. He felt ashamed. The box was crooked in the ground, the lid sloppily flung on it. The grave wasn't even very deep, and he'd been the one who buried her that way. He made a vow to himself that from then on, whoever it was, when he buried one of these House of David people, he was going to throw a bunch of flowers on top of the coffin before he threw the sand back on it.

It was lodged hard in the earth.

"I'm going to need help here," he said to the one with the wandering eye, and they all started to take off their jackets at once.

The gravedigger cleared two places wide enough to stand in, one at the head of the box and one at the foot. "I'll count to three," he said, "and then we'll lift it up to the others."

The others stood at the edge of the hole, still holding the handkerchiefs to their faces, although the gravedigger himself smelled nothing but fresh flowers now. He gripped the bottom of the box with his fingertips. His face was separated from hers by only an inch of that flimsy bit of wood.

"One, two, three," he said, but too fast for the fellow at the other end, who didn't lift, and only the head rose from the grave.

The gravedigger lowered it again.

Laura Kasischke

"Okay," he said, and then he said it slower. "One . . . two . . . three."

In a single motion they had the coffin out of the sand and the state officials rushed around and clumsily shuffled it out of the hole. The official in the grave with him crawled out in a hurry but then spent a lot of time brushing the sand off his pants, and then he put his jacket back on. Several of them had cigarettes now, and they were pacing around, and the smell of the tobacco and the smell of the death rose around the box.

No one said or did anything for several minutes. They just stared down at the loose lid. And then the leader cleared his throat and said, "Let's examine the body."

He and another one took the lid, tossed it on the ground.

Brown paper . . .

The leader put on gloves, white rubber gloves, which he'd kept in his pocket, and then they all took out white rubber gloves and put them on.

The gravedigger stood out of the way, watching, as the leader pulled a bit of the brown paper back, like peeling the skin from a piece of fruit. The others leaned in. Only one of them took out the pad of paper this time, and he began to write a few words with his pencil before stopping, shaking his head. One of the others was also shaking his head. Another gagged and glanced back at the gravedigger, and the leader motioned him toward the coffin.

Of course, he didn't want to see it. He remembered the sweetness of her lips, the waxy perfection of her skin. The teeth, brilliant in the sun. The pale red hair fanned around her.

Now the sky was fully purple, and the clouds were low and heavy, and she'd been buried for weeks. It would be nothing like the first time he'd seen her. It would be worse. She would be something else. Something no one wanted to see.

Still, they were waiting for him, so he stepped forward, and looked down.

"Is this the body you saw?"

The leader was holding the damp brown paper away from her face.

Now the eyes were closed. Her hair was pure white. She looked like someone who had lived a whole life under the ground. Grown old there. Even wise. Her hands were folded peacefully over her white dress. Her cheeks were flushed. She looked so freshly dead that it occurred to him that she was still alive.

She looked as if she had something on her mind, something she might like to tell the men assembled over her. Or something she could tell but was going to keep to herself. A secret smile on her thin lips, and the only strangeness about her at all was a trickle of black at the corner of her mouth.

The gravedigger shook his head.

"You're sure this is the grave you dug?"

He nodded.

"It couldn't have been somewhere else?"

He shook his head.

"Is this the face you saw?"

The gravedigger could say nothing, and the state officials were muttering and putting their hats back on.

He tried to remember her.

Laura Kasischke

The teeth. He'd seen her teeth, and they were dry and brilliant in the sunlight.

And the red hair. How had it turned white?

And the cheeks. The lips. He felt tired, dizzy. Yes. Something about the face was the same. Changed. But the same. He inhaled and looked at the leader, who was frowning, scowling.

"I don't know," the gravedigger said.

"You don't know?" another one said. "You can't tell the difference between an old lady and a sixteen-year-old girl?"

The gravedigger didn't answer.

"I'm going to ask you again," the leader said. "Is this the person you claim you buried in this very grave?"

The gravedigger was mesmerized by her face. The summer storm of light on it. That secret smile. He thought, *If she would only open her eyes—*

"Well? Come on now. We're all waiting. Is it? What have you got to say? You claimed you saw a young girl in this grave. Is this the young girl you claim you saw, this here old lady?"

He turned his back then and shook his head. "It . . . it might be . . ." he said.

The state officials guffawed—an explosion of annoyance and contempt. They seemed speechless with their own snorting for a while, and then they started to walk as one away from the grave, except for the leader, who stayed behind and said to the gravedigger sarcastically, "Well, then, what would you estimate the age of the deceased to be?"

"Sixty-eight," the gravedigger said. "Approximately."

The leader swore under his breath as he walked away,

too, just as it began to rain. Hard, sharp drops, and then they were running.

The gravedigger buried her again, by himself, in the rain.

We shall not all sleep. And this mystery is without controversy . . . God manifest in the flesh—not dead flesh nor corruption. He is the God of the living.

(Benjamin Purnell)

There were thirteen girls there at least when Elsie Hoover came stepping out of the shadow of a cherry tree in bloom, blinking around her. A kitten. A cow. Some creature shining with stupidity. And innocence. And she held up her hand as if to wave, and then we ran as one toward her in our white dresses, our hair flowing behind us, and one caught her by the arm, and another held her around the waist, and another grabbed hold of her silky red hair, and the little length of rope around her neck made her seem to laugh at first, in surprise, and then sing some hymn wildly for a minute before she lay down gently in her own strawberry-colored hair, a bit regretfully it seemed, in a snowy pile of pink and white petals to die.

Epilogue

Eden Springs
House of David.

He looked like a sapling on *Eden Springs' stage,*
blown around in the breeze. She had an hour
free from the concession stand and heard that
he was going to make a rare appearance, lead a prayer.
Maybe, she thought, he might glance up, see her there
when he said *Amen.*

But there were close to thirteen hundred people gathered around the stage and no way he was going to pick her
out of that crowd.

And he was a sapling, blowing, flanked by a man and a
woman dressed in white with stethoscopes hanging around
their necks. He never looked up at all. When he was done,
they helped him hobble away.

Myrtle never saw him again.

She wouldn't even bother, after a while, to glance toward the Diamond House when she passed by. He would not be on the porch. She would not glimpse him behind a window. There were rumors that he'd had a leg removed because of the diabetes, that he couldn't get out of bed because of tuberculosis, that the only people he would allow into his room were a nurse, a doctor, and the boy who read to him.

Her own life had simply gone on and seemed as if it might always go on. She lived in the Printing Shop with the brides who'd stayed. In the winter, she worked in the laundry. In the summer, she worked at the concession stand. When she saw her husband around the Colony, he was always polite, but Paul Kleinchnecht never bothered her for anything the way the other brides were bothered for dinner, money, sex, and Myrtle didn't know, but always suspected, that it was because of the baby. He knew she'd had the girl and that the girl had been taken away because she looked so much like Benjamin.

Paul Kleinchnecht, like all the others who stayed at the Colony, grew older.

There were changes.

Some were gradual.

Some happened right away.

Two months after the wedding Myrtle overheard Augusta Smith say to Violet Boruff, "I'm sick and tired of husbands. You know what? We don't have to stay here. We could get ourselves jobs in St. Joe or Benton Harbor washin' dishes. Why should we stay here, washin' dishes?"

"Because of—him."

"Benjamin? Not any of us is ever going to see him again."

Hilda Pritchard piped up then:

"I want to get a job in a dress shop! I hear that's what Lena McFarlane's doing right now. Eating steak every night, wearing jewelry."

"Well," Violet said, looking around to make sure no one else could hear. "I tell you what we do. When I was at the doctor's some weeks ago for my twisted ankle, I was approached on the sidewalk by a man who said he was a lawyer, and this lawyer says he's wantin' to talk to young girls from the House of David. That he has heard from some others. That he is building a case against Benjamin. That he will pay for the room and board of any girls willing to leave here until this case against Benjamin is brought to court."

"I want to wear scarlet," Hilda said, and Augusta laughed. "I'm damn sick of wearing white."

"I want to wear black," Violet said, "and eat me a big bloody steak every night."

After his wife ran off to Chicago with the child he'd suspected wasn't his, anyway, Dwight Baushke left the Colony and was found dead on some railroad tracks near Grand Rapids with his hair and beard all cut off, stuffed into his pockets.

The Australians, for the most part, went back to Australia. The Germans to Germany. The French to France. There were, for a decade, about six hundred Canadians—new converts who'd gotten hold of an old pamphlet in Alberta and made the journey together on a train. On the way, they sang the Negro spirituals about trains and salvation and had themselves convinced that the train was taking them straight to heaven. A large number of them died that first terrible winter of the influenza.

The young ones of the Colony became the old ones, and the new young ones wanted to hear about what it had been like when Benjamin walked among them. They'd heard he'd had a booming voice. A sense of humor. That he could be seen riding a white horse, wearing a diamond around his neck, that he had turned water into wine, that he liked Hawaiian music, that once the old man had been able to stay up all night and dance, that girls had loved him, that he'd loved girls, that he was God.

Myrtle could confirm it. She'd been there a long time. She'd known him well. They gathered around. They loved to hear her stories.

But then the Health Inspector closed the amusement park down after a boy got killed on the miniature train-tracks and there was an outbreak of something linked to the hot dogs Myrtle sold from her concession stand, and the tourists stopped coming. They opened the Whirlpool plants in Benton Harbor, and hundreds of black families moved up from the South, beside themselves with joy about their new jobs, buying houses, sending their children all dressed up in shiny shoes and plaid shirts to the brand new schools.

And then they closed the plants, and the jobs were gone.

The weeds grew up around the gate to Eden Springs,

but every spring the roses still managed to choke them out.

Lena McFarlane was sixty years old before she came back to Eden Springs, and then it was just to point the place out to her son, who only half-believed the things she'd told him about it.

"Look," she said, pointing.

They'd come a long way from California on a train, passing over the miles and through the many lives she'd had since she was a girl at the House of David—dress shop clerk, lawyer's wife, young mother, divorcée, pauper with a baby, member of a religious sect that took her and the baby along with them to Utah, defector from the sect, actress in a few small movies, secretary to the biggest banker in California—so she could show him.

She'd lived a long time.

She knew who she was.

"There," she said, and James turned.

Eden Springs was spelled out in wrought iron letters over the gateway, which looked as though no one had passed through it in decades. A vine had tightened itself around itself a hundred times, until the roses that had just begun to bloom were packed together so closely they had become one long rose.

The ticket office wasn't boarded up. No one had bothered, it seemed. It was surrounded by peonies, which must have just blossomed, sticky and feminine, festive and crawling with ants.

Lena stepped closer, and she could smell the wisteria, which was sweet and purple and seemed crazed by its own beauty. She recognized that wisteria. It hadn't changed. She knew she was seeing it at its zenith, that these were the few hours at the center of that wisteria's three days of eternity every spring.

The wisteria seemed to know it, too, and preened.

ICE CREAM was still written under the eaves. Lena could see the familiar letters behind the purple dripping.

CARAMEL CORN.

HOT DOGS.

COTTON CANDY.

COLD DRINKS.

The things people liked to buy to give themselves a treat.

On a Saturday afternoon in June.

Cool, and sweet.

Young. Alive.

Somehow, the paint had not faded, but there was no one in the Eden Springs ticket booth to sell Lena McFarlane a ticket now—although, of course, she didn't need a ticket now. The amusement park was wide open, and from where she stood looking into the brick walkways winding into the leafy distance, it seemed endless, and there was ringing in the air—a kind of high chiming—faint and silver, and Lena McFarlane stepped closer to the entrance to Eden Springs, her son considerately waiting behind her, to hear this ringing more clearly, which seemed to be coming from just the other side of the gate of wisteria and white roses, and she leaned closer.

No.

It wasn't voices.

Now she was sure—no choir of angels—but it was

like voices, light and random in the breeze, and under the sound, there was a silence like gravity, sucking the glassy bells and their delicate music in.

The End

Acknowledgments

I am indebted to R. J. Taylor for allowing me to visit the properties of the former House of David.

Without the following wonderful texts I could not have pieced together this narrative: *Brother Benjamin* by Clare E. Adkins (Andrews University Press, 1990); *The Righteous Remnant* by Robert S. Fogarty (Kent State University Press, 1982); *A Virgin's Vendetta* by Isabella Pritchard (Benton Harbor, n.d.); *The Testimony of Benjamin* (Benton Harbor, n.d.); *The What, When, Where, Why, and How of the House of David* (Benton Harbor, n.d.); *Crown of Thorns* by Francis Thorpe (Benton Harbor, 1929); *Benjamin's Last Writings* (Benton Harbor, 193-?); *The Sword of the Spirit of the House of David* (Benton Harbor, n.d.); *A Book of Remembrances* (House of David, 1931).

I am indebted to the Bentley Historical Library at the University of Michigan for providing me with most of these sources, as well as newspapers, magazines, and images—and for a lovely place to work.

Thank you to M. L. Liebler and Annie Martin for encouragement and great assistance! Thank you to Heidi Bell for her keen eye.

And most of all to Bill Abernethy, for driving me all over Michigan to do research, for buying me books, souvenirs, and all manner of interesting items from the House of David, for reading this novella in its many incarnations, and for offering his brilliant advice, which I always take.

WITHDRAWN

MADE IN MICHIGAN WRITERS SERIES

GENERAL EDITORS
Michael Delp, Interlochen Center for the Arts
M. L. Liebler, Wayne State University

ADVISORY EDITORS
Melba Joyce Boyd
Wayne State University

Stuart Dybek
Western Michigan University

Kathleen Glynn

Jerry Herron
Wayne State University

Laura Kasischke
University of Michigan

Frank Rashid
Marygrove College

Doug Stanton
Author of *In Harm's Way*

*A complete listing of the books in this series
can be found online at wsupress.wayne.edu*